THE NATURAL

"What do you want to do?" Fargo said. "Move or die?"

"I still do not know if all your guns can fire," he said.

"If I show you they can, what will you do?"

"If they all can fire," the leader said, "we would be foolish to challenge you. We would go and find easier prey."

Beyond the first three, the other Comancheros were growing restless. Fargo hoped the leader was speaking the truth. He didn't know how many men he had that would actually be willing to fire at another human being, even to save their own lives. They were, after all, only ballplayers.

"I'll have them fire," Fargo said, "but I don't know where the shots will go."

"Señor, wait—"

Fargo waved his hand and suddenly the air erupted with gunfire. Each of the baseball team fired one shot, and it sounded like a barrage, as they didn't quite all fire at the same time. . . . The Comanchero leader and his two compadres flinched at the gunfire, and drew their handguns. Fargo had his hand on his own gun. The next five seconds would determine if they would make it out of this scrape alive. . . .

THE
TRAILSMAN
#210

THE
BUSH LEAGUE

by

Jon Sharpe

Ⓢ

A SIGNET BOOK

Signet
Published by the Penguin Group
Penguin Putnam Inc., 375 Hudson Street,
New York, New York 10014, U.S.A.
Penguin Books Ltd, 27 Wrights Lane,
London W8 5TZ, England
Penguin Books Australia Ltd,
Ringwood, Victoria, Australia
Penguin Books Canada Ltd, 10 Alcorn Avenue,
Toronto, Ontario, Canada M4V 3B2
Penguin Books (N.Z.) Ltd, 182–190 Wairau Road,
Auckland 10, New Zealand

Penguin Books Ltd, Registered Offices:
Harmondsworth, Middlesex, England

Published by Signet, an imprint of Dutton NAL, a member of
Penguin Putnam Inc.

First Printing, May 1999
10 9 8 7 6 5 4 3 2 1

The first chapter of this book originally appeared in *Timber Terror*, the two
hundred ninth volume in this series.

 REGISTERED TRADEMARK—MARCA REGISTRADA

Printed in the United States of America

The Trailsman

Beginnings . . . they bend the tree and they mark the man. Skye Fargo was born when he was eighteen. Terror was his midwife, vengeance his first cry. Killing spawned Skye Fargo, ruthless, cold-blooded murder. Out of the acrid smoke of gunpowder still hanging in the air, he rose, cried out a promise never forgotten.

The Trailsman they began to call him all across the West: searcher, scout, hunter, the man who could see where others only looked, his skills for hire but not his soul, the man who lived each day to the fullest, yet trailed each tomorrow. Skye Fargo, the Trailsman, and the seeker who could take the wildness of a land and the wanting of a woman and make them his own.

Kansas City, Missouri, 1861—
where progress was creeping into the West,
along with men who were trying to use it
for their own gain . . .

1

Skye Fargo did not know the first thing about baseball and didn't want to.

"It's a big thing in the East," the man standing at the bar next to him said, "and now it looks like they want to bring it out here to the West."

"Fine with me," Fargo said, picking up his beer. "I don't have to watch it."

"No, you don't understand, Fargo," Ben Meeker said. Fargo liked Meeker, a man he had met just four days ago when he first came to Kansas City. "They're right here in Kansas City now."

"So?"

"They want to go to San Francisco."

Again, Fargo said, "So?"

"They need someone to take them."

"I told you," Fargo said, "I'm not interested in—what's it called? Baseball?"

"Right, baseball," Meeker said.

Meeker ran the livery, the stage line and, Fargo thought, had something to do with the railroad. Fargo guessed he liked the man because he was a hard worker.

"Fargo," Meeker said, "they came this far by rail, but they want to see the West. They want to go cross-country to San Francisco, and they're willing to pay someone to guide them there."

Now Fargo's interested was piqued.

"Do they have the money?"

"They'll pay very well."

"And where will they get this money they're going to use to pay very well?"

"They're gonna play baseball," Meeker said. "From town to town, city to city, they'll put on a game and charge people to come and see it."

"And people will pay for that?"

"They're payin' for it in the East," Meeker said, "and they paid for it here in Kansas City."

"When was that?" Fargo asked. "I didn't see it."

"They did it the day before you got here. You just missed it."

"Too bad."

"Are you interested?"

Fargo hesitated a moment, then said, "I'll listen to an offer from whoever's in charge."

"Fine," Meeker said. "His name's Arnold, Jack Arnold. He's over at the Silver Spur." The Spur was one of the finer hotels in town.

"He can afford to stay there?"

"He can," Meeker said, "but not all the players can. They've made other arrangements."

"Okay. And what arrangements have you made with Jack Arnold?"

Meeker looked . . . well, meek.

"I told him you'd come to the hotel to talk to him," he said.

"And what are you getting out of this, Ben?"

Meeker looked away and said, "A small finder's fee—if you take the job."

"Well," Fargo said, after a moment, "I guess there's no harm listening, and I have been here four days already. It's time for a change."

"Then I can tell him you'll see him?"

"Sure."

"Five o'clock this afternoon?"

Fargo knew it was now only about one o'clock.

"You already set the time?"

"Well . . . I'm tryin' to be helpful."

And make some extra money, Fargo knew. He laughed and shook his head.

"All right, Ben," he said, "four o'clock."

"Great." Meeker stopped facing Fargo and turned to face the bar. He waved the bartender over. "Let me buy you a beer."

"Don't you have to go over to the hotel and set this up?"

"Nope."

"You don't have to confirm it?"

Meeker ducked his head and said, "It's confirmed."

"Son of a bitch," Fargo said, chuckling, "I ought to make you buy me two beers."

At five o'clock Fargo entered the lobby of the Silver Spur Hotel. He was staying several blocks away in the less expensive—but still clean and decent—Kansas House.

He went to the desk and asked for Jack Arnold.

"I believe Mr. Arnold is in the dining room, sir."

"What's he look like?"

"Oh," said the clerk, "I think you'll know his table when you see it, sir."

Fargo shrugged and walked to the entrance to the

dining room. The clerk was right. There was one table with a lot of activity. It seemed as if Jack Arnold was holding court. He appeared to be the slightly corpulent gentleman wearing the three-piece gray suit and holding a huge cigar. There were four or five other men who seemed to be swirling around him obediently. Some of them had pads of paper and were writing furiously. Fargo correctly assumed that these were members of the press. There was one other man, looking tired and un-happy, who was seated at the table with Arnold, apparently trying to eat a meal.

Fargo walked to the table.

". . . telling you gentlemen it's going to sweep the nation. Abner Doubleday will ride this game right into the White House, mark my words."

One of the newsmen asked him a question but Arnold didn't hear him. He was looking at Fargo.

"You look like you're in fine shape, sir," Jack Arnold said as Fargo approached his table.

"Thanks," Fargo replied.

"Would you like to play ball?"

"Ball?"

"Baseball?"

"No," Fargo said, "I have no interest in baseball. Are you Jack Arnold?"

"I am, indeed, sir. What can I do for you?"

"We have a five o'clock appointment."

Arnold looked very pleased and hastily stood up, reaching for Fargo's hand, switching the cigar to his left so he could use his right.

"Skye Fargo, then?"

"That's right."

He allowed the Easterner to pump his hand enthusiastically for a while before reclaiming it. Arnold once again took hold of the cigar with his right hand.

"All right, gents, that's all for now," Arnold said. "We can talk again later."

"What kind of business do you have with the Trailsman, Mr. Arnold?" one of the men asked.

"Private business, son," Arnold said coldly. "Off with you."

The members of the press went off, buzzing among themselves about what a meeting with "Big" Jack Arnold and the Trailsman meant.

"Please, Mr. Fargo, have a seat."

Fargo sat.

"This is Mike Flowers, my manager."

"Manager?"

"He manages the baseball team," Arnold said, but Fargo still didn't know quite what that meant.

"Glad to meet you," he said, shaking hands with the man anyway. He then looked at Arnold. "I understand you want to travel overland to San Francisco."

"We do, indeed, sir, and with many stops in between. We want to see the country, and show it our wares."

Fargo refrained from asking, "What wares?" because he knew the man would just start talking about baseball again, leaving Fargo in a fog.

"I have been told that you're the man to take us on this journey."

"I am," Fargo said, "if the price is right."

Arnold sat back and puffed on his cigar. "I don't think you'll find the money a problem, sir," he said. Abruptly he looked at Flowers and said, "Mike, I'd like to conduct this business with Mr. Fargo alone, if you don't mind."

"I haven't finished eating," Flowers complained.

Arnold smiled patiently.

"There's an empty table right over there."

Flowers looked over at the table Arnold indicated, then picked up his plate and walked over to it. He sat down and resumed eating.

"The man has no social graces," Arnold said. "It's a wonder he can handle a baseball team as well as he can."

"Can he?"

"He's the best manager in the league."

Fargo had no idea what that meant, since he had no idea how many baseball teams there were. And he still wasn't sure he knew what a baseball manager was.

"Let's get down to business, Mr. Fargo," Arnold said. He took out a piece of paper and wrote down a number, then slid it over to Fargo, who looked at it. "That's for seeing us safely across country to San Francisco." He wrote another number on a different slip of paper. "That's a bonus when we get there, all in one piece. What do you think?"

Fargo looked at the two pieces of paper.

"Frankly, it's very generous, Mr. Arnold," he said. "Almost *too* generous. Are you expecting trouble?"

"With what we read about the West back East, Mr. Fargo, yes, I expect it."

"What you read is exaggerated."

"Yellow journalism?"

Fargo wasn't exactly sure what that meant but it sounded right. He didn't respond, though.

"Well, if only half of what we've read is correct, I

think we'll still need a guide. That's what the figure on the first piece of paper is for. The figure on the second is for . . . well, let's call it being a 'bodyguard.' "

"Why the slips of paper?"

"I never discuss money out loud in public," Arnold answered. "I think it's bad luck—and you never know who's listening."

Fargo looked around, but no one seemed to be listening at that moment.

"What do yo say, sir?" Arnold urged.

Fargo hesitated, then turned over one of the slips of paper Arnold had written on. He reached over, picked up the pencil Arnold had used, wrote the word yes on the paper and passed it over to the man.

2

"Excellent." Arnold beamed, indicating his apparent approval of both the answer and the method.

"When do you want to leave?" Fargo asked.

"Do you have any pressing business keeping you here?" Arnold asked.

"No," Fargo said, giving a fleeting thought to a girl he had met in town named Brenda. "No business."

"Then I can have my people ready to leave tomorrow."

"Do they have horses?"

"These are baseball players we're talking about, Mr. Fargo."

"Just Fargo."

"All right . . . Fargo. They can play ball, but most of them can't ride. We'll be taking wagons for our men, and our equipment."

"Equipment?"

"Oh, yes," Arnold said. "We have bats, balls, gloves, bases—"

"That's more than I need to know, Mr. Arnold," Fargo said, cutting the man off. "Just have your men in front of the livery stable at . . . nine A.M.?"

"Nine a.m. is acceptable," Arnold said.

"Will you be coming along?"

"No," Arnold said, "I'll be continuing on the train to San Francisco. I have a lot of publicity to do there if we're going to get the turnout we want."

Fargo looked over at Mike Flowers, who was still eating.

"So your man Flowers will be in charge?"

"Of the players," Arnold said. "You'll be in charge of the expedition."

"Will you be sure he understands that?"

"Oh, yes, sir, he will understand it. He values his job."

"I'm not looking to get him fired," Fargo said, "I just don't want any problems with the chain of command."

"There won't be any problems, Fargo," Arnold said, "I assure you."

"All right, then," Fargo said, and stood up.

"Won't you stay and have something to eat? Or a drink?" Arnold asked.

"I have some things to do if I'm going to be leaving tomorrow. What about supplies? Food, ammunition—"

"Ammunition?" Arnold said. "Oh, I think all you need is enough for yourself."

"None of these men can shoot?"

"I've never asked," Arnold said. "It hasn't even come up."

Fargo sat back down.

"Would Flowers know?"

"Maybe." Arnold waved the waiter over. "Would you ask that gentleman to rejoin us, please?"

"Yes, sir, Mr. Arnold."

From the waiter's congenial attitude, Fargo assumed that Jack Arnold was a very good tipper. The man went over and spoke to Flowers, who stood up, left his plate, and came back to the table.

"Coffee, Fargo?" Arnold asked.

Fargo agreed, since they apparently still had some things to iron out.

"Three coffees," Arnold told the waiter, "and three slices of pie."

"What kind, sir?"

"Bring out three different kinds," Arnold said. "We'll settle who gets what like men."

"Yes, sir."

As the waiter left, Arnold turned to Flowers. "Mr. Fargo has agreed to take you and the boys on to San Francisco."

"Good," Flowers said, "at least we won't get lost on the way."

"He has some questions, though."

"Shoot," the manager said.

"Exactly," Fargo said. "How many of your men can shoot?"

"Guns, you mean?"

"That's exactly what I mean."

"I think maybe three of them have military service behind them, and maybe two have hunted."

"What about you?"

"I know how to fire a gun," Flowers said, "but I wouldn't say I'm any good at it."

"All right," Fargo said. "I'll need a credit line at the general store, Mr. Arnold. We'll need supplies for the trip, and I'll want to outfit each man with a rifle."

"You've got it," Arnold said. "I did that the first

day we arrived. Just tell the owner—Mr. . . ." He looked at Flowers.

"Dennis."

"Last name?" Arnold asked.

"That's it."

"Mr. Dennis, then. He'll give you everything you need and put it on my bill."

Fargo knew that the general store carried fine rifles and crate loads of ammunition.

"All right, then," he said, "we're going to need . . . what, six rifles?"

"You said you wanted to outfit every man?" Flowers asked.

"That's right," Fargo said. "How many men are on a baseball team?"

"Well," Flowers said, "when they're on the field there's nine of them, and of course the pitcher might need to be replaced . . . that's ten, maybe more . . ."

"Wait a minute," Fargo said, "just tell me how many rifles I'm going to have to buy to outfit everybody on the . . ."

"Team." Flowers finished for him, closing his eyes. He did some quick math, then looked at Fargo and said, "Well, counting me . . . twenty-six should do it."

After a moment of stunned silence Fargo said, "What? There's twenty-five men on this team?"

"Well," Arnold said, "we're traveling with twenty-five because we're putting on exhibitions."

"What do you mean?"

"Did you see the game we played here the other day?" Arnold asked.

"No," Fargo said, "I got here the day after."

"Well, we put on a game, which means we have

to put two teams on the field . . . I take it you don't much know anything about baseball?"

"Not a thing."

"Well, it takes two teams of nine men to start a game. At any time during the game someone might have to be replaced. We need to carry enough men to field two teams and have enough replacements."

"Twenty-five," Flowers reiterated, "and me."

"Twenty-six."

"Correct," Arnold confirmed.

"How many wagons do you have?"

"We thought three would be enough."

"Eight men a wagon? With supplies? I don't think so," Fargo said. "What we're talking about here now is a damned wagon train. You need a wagon master."

Fargo turned to Flowers.

"How many men can drive a team?"

"Oh," Flowers said, "half a dozen or so."

Well, that's something, Fargo thought.

"Can anyone cook?"

Flowers frowned, then said, "No."

"You're going to need a cook," Fargo said to Arnold.

"Hire one."

"And probably some extra men."

"Hire them."

"This is going to cost more money."

"Do it," Arnold said. "I'll even raise your fee."

"I think you better," Fargo said, although he noticed Flowers didn't look too happy about it.

"Can you get the men, supplies, and extra wagons by tomorrow morning?" Arnold asked.

"I don't know," Fargo said, "it's pretty late in the day to be looking for men."

"The saloons are full of them, aren't they?" Arnold asked.

"We're talking about good men," Fargo said, "men I can count on, and maybe even trust."

"Do you know such men?"

"No," Fargo said, thinking of Meeker, "but I might know someone who does."

"I tell you what," Arnold said. "Later this evening I will be at the Kansas State Theater listening to the lovely Miss Brenda Benet sing. After that I intend to go to the State Street Saloon right across the street for an after-dinner drink. Why don't you meet me there about nine tonight and let me know if you've done it?"

"All right." Fargo agreed, having already made acquaintances with the saloon the previous night.

"If you don't have everything you need by that time, we'll put off departure for another day."

"How do I let my players know?" Flowers asked. "They'll be asleep."

"At nine o'clock?" Fargo asked.

"Curfew," Flowers said.

"Mr. Flowers is under the impression that his players actually keep his curfew," Arnold said. He looked at the manager. "You can make sure they know, Mike. Don't worry about it."

"This all seems a little slipshod," Flowers said.

"Well," Fargo said, annoyed that he was defending himself, "I didn't know you had twenty-six men."

"Not your fault, Fargo," Arnold said. "Mr. Flowers was referring to me. I sometimes get carried away with my enthusiasm and let the small details get away from me."

"Small details?" Flowers huffed.

"You see," Arnold went on, "money is my . . . well, you might even call it a talent."

"He thinks money can buy anything," Flowers said.

"Oh, I don't think it, Mike," Arnold said, grinning widely, "I know it." He looked at Fargo. "You wave enough money in front of the storekeeper's face and he'll get you everything you need. The same holds true for the liveryman."

Fargo hated to admit it, but in this case he thought Arnold was right.

"Perhaps you'd like some cash instead of credit?" Arnold asked. He started to reach for his wallet.

"Don't do that!" Fargo snapped.

Arnold stopped in midmotion.

"I beg your pardon?"

"Don't wave money at me in here," Fargo said. "Credit will be fine."

"Very well, then," Arnold said, sitting back in his chair. "Are we clear on the plan so far?"

"We're clear," Fargo replied.

"Good," Arnold said. "I'll see you at nine, then."

"Will you be there?" Fargo asked Flowers.

"Don't like the theater," the man said. "I'm at a boardinghouse at the south end of town with the team. Mrs. Sunderly's. You can come and tell me what happens, if you like."

"I'll do that," Fargo said, and then added, "before I go and see Mr. Arnold."

He thought he saw a small smile tug at the lips of the baseball manager.

3

Jack Arnold was certainly right about Dennis, the storekeeper. As soon as Fargo mentioned Arnold's name, the man was willing to give him anything.

"I need twenty-six Winchesters."

"You got 'em," Dennis said, without flinching. "Tomorrow morning."

Now Dennis flinched.

"That might be hard."

"How many can you get me by tomorrow."

"Maybe . . . fifteen."

Fargo didn't like the idea of traveling all the way from Kansas City to San Francisco with unarmed men along.

"How many Colts?"

"What model?"

"Just handguns," Fargo said. "How many?"

Dennis thought for a moment, then said, "I could make up the difference in handguns."

Of course, if we need to do any shooting at a distance, the handguns would be useless, Fargo thought.

"But I could get you the Winchesters by day after tomorrow."

"How?"

"I'll send somebody to Jefferson City," Dennis

said. "I have another store there. They can make it there and back in time."

"All right," Fargo said, "let's do it that way, then."

Dennis wrote down the order for twenty-six rifles.

"All right, then," Fargo said, "I need enough of the following for twenty-seven men—coffee, bacon, beans, canned fruit . . ."

Dennis happily kept taking notes.

When Fargo was finished with the general store, he went looking for Meeker. The man owned the livery, but didn't work there. At this time of day— after five, now—he knew that Meeker would either be eating, or drinking, or both.

He found him at a small tavern called the Dutchman's Saloon.

"There you are," Meeker exclaimed. "Do I owe you another beer?"

"I'll buy *you* one."

"You took the job?"

"I did," Fargo said, "though I think I'm going to regret it."

"Why's that?"

Fargo had been in the Dutchman before. He held two fingers up to the bartender, who knew what he meant.

"Do you know how many men are on a baseball team?" Fargo asked.

Meeker shrugged.

"Nine? Ten?"

"Twenty-five on this one, and a manager by the name of Flowers."

"Flowers?" Meeker said, laughing.

"I've got to outfit every one of them, even though most of them don't know how to shoot."

"Why do they need to know how to shoot?" Meeker asked. "Anybody see you traveling with all those men—Indians, outlaws, Comancheros—even if they're just *carrying* a gun, they're gonna think twice."

"Twenty-six tenderfeet, Ben." Fargo sighed.

"Is the money good?"

Fargo looked at Meeker and said, "The money is *real* good."

"I knew it would be," Meeker said smugly. "Do you even know who Jack Arnold is?"

"No."

"J and A Steel, the Arnold Mills, Arnold Publishing—books and newspapers—"

"Okay, so I know he's got money and he made it all in the East. Why's he so excited about baseball?"

"From what I hear," Meeker said, "it's because he likes to play it."

Fargo thought of the corpulent Arnold playing anything—even horseshoes—and had to laugh.

"Oh yeah, I hear he gets out there and plays—and they wear these uniforms that look like pajamas . . ."

"No."

"Yup. And these odd caps . . ."

"Do you think this baseball thing will ever catch on the way Arnold is telling the press?" Fargo asked.

"Have your read his quotes in the press?"

"No, but he was surrounded by newspaper reporters when I met him at his hotel."

"Well, he's been playin' this up in Eastern newspapers—most of them his—for months, and now he's doin' it in the West."

"I just can't see it," Fargo said, as the bartender put two beers in front of them.

"Cold ones," the bartender said, nodding.

"Thanks."

Counting those two, Fargo had heard the Dutchman bartender say six words of English—"What?" "More?" and "Two bits," filled out the rest of his vocabulary.

"You haven't seen the game played, though," Meeker said to Fargo after taking a long sip.

"No."

"People here liked it."

"You're kidding!"

"I'm not. The *kids* especially loved it."

"What about you?"

"Me? I thought it was pretty silly, myself . . . but if there's a way to make money in it, I'm all for it."

"What'll we have out here next?" Fargo asked. "Tea parties?"

"I hear they have them in some of the bigger hotels in Denver."

"Now I know you're lying."

"I swear!"

"Well," Fargo said, "I think there's definitely a way for you to make money in this—as if you didn't already know."

"Arnold's credit is good with me," Meeker said. "He's already bought three wagons."

"We'll need three more."

"All right!"

"And teams for each of them."

"You'll need them . . . by when?"

"Morning after tomorrow?"

"I can do it."

Fargo shook his head. "I'm a goddamned wagon master."

"Gettin' paid like one?"

"You're damned right I am." Fargo smiled.

Over the next round of beers, Fargo questioned Meeker about a cook and a couple of hands to ride with him.

"I'm going to need some men I can count on to know what they're doing."

"I know somebody who can cook," Meeker offered.

"Who?"

Meeker inclined his head toward the bartender.

"The Dutchman?" Fargo asked.

"Yup."

"He doesn't serve food here."

"Don't matter," Meeker said. "He can cook."

"On the trail?"

"He *wants* to go out on the trail," Meeker said. "Says he's goin' stir-crazy here."

"He'd sell this place?"

"No," Meeker said, shaking his head, "he'll come back here. He just wants—ya know, a vacation."

"I've only heard him say six words of English," Fargo said. "I know 'cause I've counted. Can he speak English well?"

"When he wants to."

"What's his name, anyway?"

"Just call him Dutchman."

"Hey, Dutchman!" Fargo called to him.

The man hurried over.

"I'm outfitting a small party—well, not a small party, a small wagon train—to go from here to San Francisco. I need a cook."

"I cook."

"Do you cook well?"

"I cook good."

"Can you be ready to leave day after tomorrow?"

"Sure, I leave."

"Do you want to know the pay?"

"You Fargo," the Dutchman said, "you pay fair."

Meeker smiled at Fargo and said, "Looks like you got yourself a cook."

Meeker left Fargo and the Dutchman and went to take care of his order for wagons and horses. He also told Fargo he'd find him two men.

"Men I can *trust*," Fargo added.

Meeker rubbed his jaw thoughtfully and said, "That'll be a little harder," then laughed and left.

Fargo nursed a beer at a back table, wondering if he was really making a mistake. Still, Meeker had a point. Taking that many men across country should be safe enough, unless they ran into an honest-to-God war party. He'd have to put a man with a gun on the seat of each wagon, even if the damned fools didn't know how to fire them.

Also, it might be interesting for a while, talking to some men from back East—and he never had seen a baseball game. He wondered what that would be like.

In the end, it was his curiosity that made him take and keep the job, and his boredom at being in one place for too long.

Tonight he would have to explain it to Brenda Benet.

Brenda Benet was a singer, and—if Skye Fargo was any judge—a damned good one. She was on a nationwide tour that would have her singing in Kansas City for the next two weeks. She'd been hoping after their first night together that Fargo would stay in Kansas City for the duration. He had told her that he doubted it, that he hardly ever stayed in one place that long. She'd taken it as a challenge and, since they were naked at the time, set about to try to give him a good reason to stay.

However, as much as he loved beautiful women, he was ready to leave Kansas City.

After all, there were beautiful women all over the country. How often did a Jack Arnold come along with a wide-open wallet?

4

When Ben Meeker returned to the Dutchman's Saloon, he had four men in tow. Each spoke with Fargo in turn and when they had all gone, Meeker sat down with him.

"No good?"

Fargo shook his head. "Were they the best you could find?"

"For tonight they were," Meeker said. "Tomorrow, during the day, I'll probably be able to do better for you."

"I hope so," Fargo said.

"Are you takin' this one just because I asked you to?" Meeker asked.

"No," Fargo said, without hesitation, "I don't think we've become that close yet, Ben. Why?"

"Oh," Meeker said, "if it turns out, well, badly, I don't want you comin' back to me with the blame."

"Oh," Fargo said, "I sure as hell will do that. We are *that* close, at least."

At eight-thirty, Fargo walked to the south end of town and found the rooming house where the baseball players were staying. He mounted the front porch and knocked. He was surprised when Mike Flowers himself answered.

"Landlady's asleep," he explained, "I didn't want you to wake her. We can talk out here."

He closed the door behind him. That suited Fargo just fine.

"How'd you know I'd come?" he asked.

"You struck me this afternoon as a man who does what he says," Flowers replied. "I'm glad I was right. Gives me confidence for the trip."

"Let's talk about the trip, Mr. Flowers."

"Just Mike," the man said, "or Skipper."

"Skipper?"

"That's what the players all call me," Flowers explained, "Skipper, or Skip. Like the captain of a boat."

"I see," Fargo said, though he really didn't see the connection.

There were a couple of chairs on the porch, and they sat down in them to talk further.

"Are we leaving in the morning?" Flowers asked.

"No," Fargo said, "the day after. It'll take me that long to get the rifles."

Flowers shook his head.

"I knew we'd need bats for every man, but it never occurred to me we'd need rifles."

"You seemed annoyed earlier today, when the subject got around to money," Fargo noted.

"Oh," Flowers sighed. "Jack's got plenty of money for all kinds of supplies, and to hire you and some others. When it comes to the players, however—well, that's where he cuts corners." Flowers spread his arms. "That's why we're all staying here."

"All of you?"

Flowers nodded.

"This place doesn't look big enough . . ."

"Four to a room," Flowers said. "I'm actually glad Jack gave in to you on the subject of extra wagons. We were going to be stuffed into those wagons like sardines. Maybe now we'll have a little more room."

"Is he sending you overland to save on train tickets?" Fargo asked. "Seems to me this is much more expensive."

"No, he's not cutting corners there," Flowers said. "He actually wants us to travel through the West and play some games. Introduce the people of the West to baseball."

"What do *you* think about this game, Mike?"

"I thought it would be popular in the East, and it is, very much so," Flowers said. "I have my doubts about the West, though—except I think it may go over well in California."

Fargo studied Flowers for a few moments. The man did not seem to be without the social graces Jack Arnold said he was lacking. He was also not as morose as he was earlier, in the presence of the wealthy man.

"You don't like Jack Arnold very much, do you?" Fargo asked.

"Just between you and me?"

"Definitely."

"I despise him—but he's the kind of man who is going to be good for the game, in general."

"I understand he likes to play."

Flowers grinned.

"You've done your homework. Yeah, he likes to play—can't, but likes to."

"So you let him?"

Flowers shrugged. "He owns the team."

"But you run it?"

"Yeah," Flowers said wryly, "I run it—when he lets me."

"Why work for him, then?"

"Because I can't get a job anywhere else where I'd make as much money," Flowers said. "I've got a wife and kids back East, Fargo, and they've gotten into a bad habit. They like to eat."

Fargo couldn't fault the man's motives there, not with a family to feed.

"I'll let the players know that we're leaving the morning after next," Flowers said.

"How are they going to feel about me?"

"They'll do what you tell them to do, after I explain the situation."

"That's good."

"We've got a couple who are kind of full of themselves," Flowers went on. "You might have to earn their respect."

Great, Fargo thought, *just what I need*.

"You know, Jack was right about one thing today," Flowers said.

"What?"

"You are in good shape," the manager said, "tall and rangy. I bet I could make a decent pitcher out of you."

"I don't even know what that means," Fargo said, "but thanks, anyway."

Fargo stood up, and Flowers followed.

"You know," he said, "I can't wait until you see the game for the first time."

He extended his hand and Fargo shook it.

"I'm not much for games."

Flowers smiled. "We'll see, won't we?"

"Yep, I guess we will."

They walked to the steps.

"Going to talk to Arnold now?" Flowers asked.

"That's right."

"Remember, I was the one who said he's good for the game."

"Don't worry," Fargo said, "nothing that passed between you and me will reach him. That's a promise."

"I appreciate it," Flowers said. "I was being frank with you."

"Well, I appreciate that," Fargo said, "and I'll try to extend you the same courtesy."

Fargo got to the State Street Saloon well ahead of Jack Arnold. He knew from personal experience just when Brenda Benet's show ended. He also knew he'd have to get a table early, because the place filled up after the show. He knew all this because it was at the State Street Saloon that he had first met Brenda, after seeing her show.

The saloon looked like some of the theaters Fargo had been in in Washington City. No gambling, no saloon girls, just a lot of leather and mahogany. No cowboys in here, just theater-goers and enthusiasts.

He ordered a beer from the bar, commandeered a table in the back, and settled down to wait for Arnold.

When the doors opened and a swarm of men entered, Fargo knew that Jack Arnold would be at the center of the group. Sure enough, the mob found a table and sent one of their numbers to the bar for drinks. That was when Fargo saw Arnold, and apparently, Arnold saw him at the exact same time. The man excused himself from his party and came over. Fargo gave him credit for not simply sitting down and trying to force Fargo to come to him.

"Good evening, Fargo."

"Mr. Arnold."

"Good news, or bad?"

"A mixture, I'm afraid," Fargo told him, and gave him the story.

"All right, then," Arnold said when Fargo was done, "you'll be leaving day after tomorrow. Anything else?"

"I haven't hired the other men, yet," Fargo said. "Do I have a free hand for that, since we're so close to our departure time?"

"Of course, of course," Arnold said, waving a hand. "You have more experience in these matters."

"Yes, I do. About paying them—"

"Pay them what you think they're worth."

"I will be needing some cash for that."

Arnold looked around, then sat down and took out his wallet. Fargo didn't stop him this time. The man took some cash from his wallet with a minimum of fanfare and slid it across the table to Fargo.

"Enough?"

Fargo pocketed it and said, "Oh, I think it'll be enough."

"Why don't you come over to the table and join us? I can introduce you to the mayor, and the—"

"That's all right," Fargo interrupted, holding up his hand. "I'm fine right here. I'll finish this beer and be on my way."

"Sure I can't change your mind?" Arnold asked.

"Miss Benet will be joining us as soon as she changes her clothes."

"Thanks, anyway."

"Extraordinary woman," Arnold exhaled, shaking his head. "I don't mind telling you I'm hoping to entice her into my bed tonight."

"With money?"

"What else?" Arnold asked, patting his rounded belly. "I don't have much else to work with, do I?"

"Oh, I think you do," Fargo said.

"No, no," Arnold said, "money is my virtue, Fargo, as well as my weapon. It's also my friend."

"I can think of some other words for it."

"Like what?"

"Captor," Fargo said, "maybe even prison."

"Money, a prison?" Arnold asked. He stood up and stared down at Fargo. "I don't think you'd say that if you had some of it, Fargo."

"And I don't think I ever will, Mr. Arnold," Fargo replied. "And you know what? I'm just fine with that."

"Money's like the perfect woman or the perfect wine, Fargo," Arnold said. "Once you've had it, you find it hard to live without."

"Then I'm glad I never had it," Fargo answered. "That way I don't know what I'm missing."

"My friend," Arnold said, turning away, "you sure don't."

5

Fargo went to his hotel to wait. He knew that Jack Arnold was going to be disappointed tonight in his hope of getting Brenda Benet into his bed. He was not her type, money and all.

He removed his boots and his shirt, and hung his gunbelt on the bedpost. He reclined that way on the bed, hands behind his head, waiting, going over the day's events in his mind, projecting the events of the coming days and wondering, once again, if his curiosity and boredom were going to get him in trouble.

Finally, there was a knock at the door. He walked to the door in his bare feet, and opened it.

"Oh God!" Brenda said, exploding into the room. "I just spent an hour too long with the most infuriating man!"

Her violet eyes were flashing and her impressive cleavage was heaving.

"How long did you spend with him?"

"An hour," she said, removing her wrap in a huff, "which was, as I said, an hour too long. Do you believe he thought he could *buy* me for the night?"

"Shocking."

"Why do rich men think they can buy every-thing?"

"Because usually they can?" Fargo replied.

"Well, not this man," she said. "He couldn't buy *this* woman."

"Whereas," Fargo said with a smile, "I get you for free?"

She turned and looked at him, then grinned and said, "Oh, yes. You can't believe how being in the presence of a man like that makes you that much more appealing to me." She reached behind her back to slowly undo her dress, which caused her breasts to jut out toward him. "I'm on fire," she crooned, dropping her dress to the floor and step-ping out of it. She was a full-bodied woman, with fleshy hips and a well-padded rear, her skin as pale and smooth as porcelain—but with none of that substance's coolness.

He stood still as she undid his pants, sliding them down his legs along with his underwear. He stepped out of both garments and she tossed them away. She ran her hands over his broad chest, kissed his nipples, then sank to her knees in front of his manhood, cooing to it.

"You have the prettiest parts," she said to him. "Have I told you that before?"

"You have."

"Well, you still do," she said, abruptly taking him fully into her mouth.

He rocked back in bliss, until he was rising up on his toes from the effort it took not to explode into her mouth.

"Lie down," she commanded, as she let him slide

free of her mouth. She pushed him back so that he fell onto the bed.

As he did so, she climbed onto the bed with him, pressing herself to him, straddling him. He reached for her big, beautiful breasts, palming them, squeezing and flicking her dusky nipples with his thumbs. Gasping for breath, she reached between their bodies, took hold of him, and slid him into her. They both gasped this time as he filled her up, her heat enveloping him. She began to move on him, riding him up and down with her hands flat against his chest, her head tossed back, and her hair cascading down her back and shoulders. The room filled with the sound of their quickened breathing. Finally she shuddered and cried out, and he roared as he erupted into her. She kept on bucking, looking for more and more until he had no more to give, and then she collapsed on him.

"Too fast," she gasped, "too fast, but I needed that, oh Lord, how I *needed* that . . ."

He slid his hands over her body, caressing her back, and said, "There's more where that came from."

She laughed and said, "Oh, I know that . . ."

Later they made love again, but slower this time, sweeter. . . .

She moaned as his lips and tongue explored her, kissing and licking her breasts and nipples, taking as much of her into his mouth as he could, and then continuing down over her soft, smooth belly until his mouth was pressed between her legs, his tongue was working avidly.

"Oh God, oh God, yes," she gasped, pressing herself into his face, lifting her buttocks from the bed, "yes, yes, ooh, like that, Skye, darling, right there, oh God . . ."

It didn't take long for her to climax and then he mounted her quickly, sliding easily into her. As hot as her skin was, inside she was an inferno. He slid his hands beneath her to cup her big buttocks as she implored him to take her harder. He fell into a lustful rhythm, banging into her as hard as she asked, and harder still, the bed bouncing off of the floor, the bedpost knocking against the wall until finally he exploded again inside of her.

"Day after tomorrow?" she repeated sadly, when he told her he'd be leaving. "Why so soon?"

"I took a job."

"Doing what?"

"Guiding some people to San Francisco."

"And you'd rather do that than stay here with me?" She pouted.

"Yes," he said, without hesitation.

She slapped him on the shoulder, then reached over and playfully bit him there.

"You're a horribly, horribly honest man, Skye Fargo, the only one I think I've ever met."

"And you don't hate me for it?"

"No," she said. "I wish you'd lie a little this time about missing me, but no, I don't hate you."

"I will miss you."

"Liar." She cuddled up closer to him. "When will you be in San Francisco?"

"I'm not sure, yet."

"I think we're finishing our tour there," she said. "Maybe we'll be there at the same time."

"Maybe," he said. "That would be . . . nice."

She sighed sleepily and said, "I don't even mind if you're lying. It *would* be nice."

He wasn't lying. It would be nice to spend a few more days with her in San Francisco.

He wondered if she'd hate him, though, when she found out whom he was working for.

In the morning, Brenda rose first, as she had the past few days, kissed him, and left. She'd sleep most of the day, so that when she went on stage there would be no bags under her eyes.

Fargo stayed in bed another half hour then got up himself, washed, and dressed, then went down to have breakfast in the hotel dining room. He was halfway finished with his steak and eggs when Ben Meeker came in, spotted him, and walked to his table.

"You're early," Fargo said.

"What are you talkin' about?" Meeker asked. "It's already eight-thirty. I've a business to run, my friend, and I've been up for hours."

"Had breakfast?"

"Yes," Meeker replied, "but that doesn't mean I can't have more. I'll just have some coffee and one of your biscuits with some marmalade."

"Help yourself."

"Thanks, I will."

"Are you going to find me those two men today?" Fargo asked.

"Without a doubt," Meeker said. "Town like this there's bound to be two reliable men."

"Oh, hell . . ." Fargo said.

"What?"

"I forgot to tell the Dutchman that we'll be leaving *tomorrow* morning and not *this* morning."

"Don't worry about it," Meeker said. "I happen to know he rises early, and when you're not there bangin' on his door, he'll know."

"I'll talk to him when I'm done here," Fargo said. "He's going to have to buy some pots and pans and other gear for the trip."

"He'll love that."

Meeker finished smearing a biscuit with marmalade and then stuffed the entire thing into his mouth. He washed it down with a slurp of coffee, which he didn't even blow on to try and cool it off.

"I'm glad you're not coming on this trip," Fargo said.

"Why's that?"

"Because I'd hate to see you do that every day."

Meeker finished swallowing and then said, "I learned to eat in a hurry so I don't waste any of the day."

"I think if you just take everything slow, you'll find it doesn't go to waste."

"I'm afraid I'm too old a dog for that," Meeker said. "I don't have a slow speed in me. Gotta go, anyway. If I don't check in at the livery, that lazy bum I pay to open for me will open late."

"Find me those men."

"Consider them found, my friend," Meeker said. He paused then, regarding Fargo with his hands on his hips.

"What?" Fargo asked.

"I'm just sorry you'll be leaving Kansas City so early," Meeker said. "I feel that we became friends very quickly."

"I feel the same way."

"But friends come and go," Meeker said, sadly.

"I don't agree," Fargo said. "Not the good ones. They're around forever."

"I hope you're right, Fargo," Meeker said. "Hey, I'll see you later."

The man turned and nearly fled from the room, almost knocking over a couple who had just entered the dining room. He tossed an apology over his shoulder without looking back. Fargo wondered what it must be like to have that much energy. Meeker was almost forty, yet he seemed to be as lively as a twenty-year-old.

6

Fargo didn't have time to get out of the dining room before somebody else came looking for him. This time it was Mike Flowers, the baseball manager. He was wearing an Eastern style suit, and Fargo decided to find out if any of these baseball players had some decent trail clothes. He didn't want to travel with twenty-six men who wore suits and ties every day.

"I'm glad I caught you," Flowers said.

"I just finished my breakfast," Fargo replied, "but can I offer you a cup of coffee?"

"That's okay, I had some," Flowers said, but he sat down anyway.

"What can I do for you?"

"I thought you might want to meet the boys before we started our trip," Flowers said. "Give them a chance to meet you, too."

"Might not be a bad idea," Fargo agreed.

"Good, then you can come to practice."

"To what?"

"Practice. I'm going to have the team do some practicing today."

"They still have to practice?" Fargo asked. "Don't they know how to play yet?"

Flowers laughed.

"Yeah, they do, but in order to stay sharp you have to work out, and practice. What about you? Can you shoot that gun on your hip well?"

"Well enough."

"Don't you practice?"

"No."

"Why not?"

"Because I don't draw it unless I have to," Fargo said, "and then it's always in self-defense."

Flowers stared at him for a few moments, then waved his hand and said, "Okay, bad comparison. Anyway, if you come to the open area at the south end of town where we set up the field for the game the other day, you'll get a chance to see just what baseball is."

"So you're inviting me to this practice."

"Right."

"I'll be there," Fargo said. "Maybe then I can stop sounding so dumb about this game."

"Most of the people here in the West are dumb about it until they see it," Flowers said. "I'll be anxious to see what you think."

"Okay, then, when is this practice going to take place?"

"In about an hour. We'll probably go through the motions for the first hour, and then have us a simulated game."

"What kind of game?" Fargo asked with a puzzled look on his face.

"A . . . practice game. Just come and see what we're doing, okay?"

"Sure."

"Thanks, Fargo," Flowers said. "I appreciate it."

As Flowers laughed, Fargo marveled at what a different man the baseball manager was when he wasn't around his boss, Jack Arnold.

Fargo went by the general store to check in with Mr. Dennis about the rifles.

"My man has left already," Dennis said. "Tell Mr. Arnold they'll be here this evening."

"Arnold may be paying you," Fargo said to the man, "but these weapons have to pass my inspection before you get your money. You have to satisfy me, understand?"

"Sure thing, Mr. Fargo," Dennis said nervously, "sure thing. I'm sure you'll be satisfied with the merchandise."

"And don't forget the extra rounds," Fargo said.

"You'll have 'em."

Fargo was thinking what a good idea practice was, and it was good that these men were used to doing it, because he was going to have them practice long and hard with the rifles.

From there, he went to the livery, where he found Ben Meeker chewing out his employee for opening the door five minutes late. When Meeker saw Fargo, he dismissed the young man and came over to talk to him.

"Haven't had time to find those men, but I'll be gettin' on it."

"I'm not here about that."

"What then?"

"My Ovaro," Fargo said. "I want him checked over. I want to be sure he's in shape to travel first thing tomorrow morning."

"I'll have my man—"

"No," Fargo cut him off, "either you do it, or I'll do it myself."

"Say no more," Meeker said. "I'll handle it myself, personally."

"Thanks, Ben."

"Sure thing. Where are you off to now?"

"I'm going to go and watch a baseball game," Fargo said, "or a practice game, or something. I'm just going to get an idea of what it's all about."

"That's a good idea," Meeker said. "Let me know what you think."

"I will."

He left the livery and headed for the south end of town.

When he got there, he saw a bunch of men in white running around, chasing a small white ball, or trying to hit it with a stick. At least, that's what it looked like to him.

Some stands had been set up for the game that had been played the day before he arrived, and they hadn't been taken down yet. He sat on the lowest level to watch.

Mike Flowers spotted him, yelled some instructions to the men, and then came over to sit with him.

"You're just in time," he said. "We're going to start a game."

"Good."

"Do you know anything about it at all?"

"No, nothing."

"Good, then I'll start from the beginning," Flowers said. "There are nine men on a team. One team takes the field and the other team is at bat. The 'bat'

is the rounded stick you see some of the boys holding. See that man standing out there, throwing the
ball in to the, uh, catcher?"

"The catcher . . . that's the guy squatting down
and catching the ball?"

"Right. The man throwing it to him is the pitcher.
He 'pitches' the ball in to the catcher. There'll be a
man standing at the plate—there's usually a wide
'plate' on the ground—and the pitcher must throw
the ball across the plate. The batter—the man holding the bat—is going to try and hit the ball. When he
does, he'll run to first base—that's over there. If he
can, he'll try to run as far as he can go . . . second
base . . . third base . . . or even all the way home."

"Home?"

"It's called 'home plate.' "

"Oh."

"The idea is to hit the ball, run the bases, and for
each man who touches home plate, you get a 'run.'
The team with the most runs wins."

"I see."

"Do you?"

"No."

"Okay," Flowers said, "let's just watch for a
while."

"Okay," Fargo replied, and they watched.

Along the way Fargo asked questions when they
occurred to him, and was encouraged by Flowers to
do so.

"Why isn't the pitcher letting the batter hit the
ball?"

Flowers explained that it was the pitcher's job to
get the batter "out." He could do that by striking
him out, or by getting him to hit the ball to one of

the men on the field. A "strikeout" was when the ball came over the plate three times without being hit, or when the batter swung three times and missed, or a combination of the two.

Fargo was sorry he asked.

Later, when a man walked from the plate to first base without hitting the ball, Fargo asked why. Flowers explained it was because the pitcher had "missed" the plate eight times before getting three strikes.

"It's called a walk."

"Why don't the batters just wait each time? Then they can each walk and a run will come around."

"If they don't swing and the ball comes across the plate, it's a strike . . . remember I told you that?"

"I remember," Fargo lied.

"Any other questions?"

"No."

"Let's keep watching."

"How long does this go on?"

"Well, sometimes it varies, but we're starting to make the games nine innings now."

"What's an inning?"

Flowers started to explain, and again Fargo was sorry he asked.

Finally, one side claimed victory over the other by a "score" or "count" of eight to five.

"That means the winning team had eight men cross the plate, and the losing team had five," Flowers explained.

"Uh-huh."

"What did you think?"

"It's . . . kind of complicated."

"Not when you've watched it enough."

"Tell me something," Fargo asked. "Why don't the batters just hit the ball out of the other men's reach?"

"Well, they're trying to do that . . ."

"And why do they swing a miss?"

"What?"

"I've seen some of them miss," Fargo said. "Is that a strategy?"

Flowers laughed.

"No, they're trying to hit the ball, just sometimes they can't."

"That must by why you make them practice."

"Well, yes, but . . . they can't hit the ball every time."

"Why not?" Fargo asked. "It doesn't look that hard, if they're keeping their eye on it."

"You don't think it looks hard?"

Fargo stared at Flowers and said, "Well, no . . . is it suppose to be?"

"Would you like to try?"

"Oh . . . I don't think so . . ."

"Why? You said it doesn't look hard. I'll get you a bat. You stand up there and hit the ball whenever you think you can."

"Do I have to swing every time?"

"No, sometimes the ball will be outside, or inside, or not where you want to swing at it. It's up to the umpire to decide if you should have swung at it. If he thinks you should, he'll call it a strike. If not, it's a ball. Eight balls, and you go to first base."

"I think I'd rather hit it," Fargo said.

"Then give it a try."

"Mike, I really don't—"

"I'll tell the boys. I'll introduce you first, and then we'll get you a bat."

"Mike—" Fargo complained, but Flowers was already trotting over to the players, gathering them around and telling them that they were going to meet Skye Fargo, who said that hitting the ball didn't look so hard.

After that, he didn't have much of a choice.

7

Flowers came back to the stands for Fargo and said, "Here," as he tossed him a baseball. "Thought you'd like to see what you're gonna try and hit. The boys are ready for you."

"Mike," Fargo said, turning the ball over in his hand. "It's pretty hard."

"Yeah, it is."

"This might not be the right way for me to meet these fellas, Mike."

Flowers looked out onto the field—which Fargo noticed was in the shape of a diamond—and then back at Fargo.

"You want to back out?"

"No," Fargo answered sternly, "I don't want to back out . . ." It occurred to him that if he did, he might lose the respect of these twenty-five men before he ever gained it. His big mouth had gotten him into this, so now he had to go through with it.

"Okay," he said defiantly, "let's do it."

"Uh, you might want to let me hold on to your gun."

"My gun?"

"Might get in your way."

Fargo looked around. He didn't know any of

these men, but none of them were armed. The "uniforms" they were wearing didn't even seem to have pockets.

"It's okay, Fargo," Flowers said.

"Well," Fargo replied, "just for a short time."

Fargo undid the gunbelt and handed it to Flowers, who slung it over his shoulder. Together they walked to home plate.

"Fargo, this is Vince Hogan," Flowers said, introducing him to a big man with a thick neck and bulky arms. "He's our best home run hitter."

"Home run?" Fargo queried.

"That's when you hit the ball so far that nobody can get it, and you trot around the bases," Hogan said. "Everybody calls me Basher."

The man put out his hand and Fargo shook it. The grip was the hardest he'd ever encountered, and yet Basher was not trying to crush his hand.

"I'll show you how to hold the bat," Basher offered.

"Thanks."

It took only a few minutes to show Fargo the proper grip, once they decided he was a right-handed hitter.

"Now, see that pitcher out there?" Basher said.

"I see him."

The pitcher, unlike Basher, was tall and lithe.

"The first thing he's gonna do is throw the ball at your head."

"Why's he going to do that?"

"To try and intimidate you. He won't be tryin' to hit you, just tryin' to get close enough to make you duck, or to knock you down."

"So what do I do?"

"Stand your ground," Basher advised, "and glare at him."

"Thanks for the advice."

"After that," Basher said, "he'll throw the ball over the plate as hard as he can."

"And what do I do then?"

"Hit it," Basher said, "as far as you can. These fellas all laughed when they heard that you said it didn't look hard. To most people, hitting a baseball is the hardest thing in the world."

"Is it to you?"

"Naw," Basher replied, grinning, "to me it's easy. Just keep your eye on it and swing as hard as you can."

That's what I thought, Fargo told himself, though he didn't say it out loud.

"Go ahead, Mr. Fargo," Basher said, handing him the bat, "give it a go."

"Thanks."

"Swing the bat a few times," the man added, "just to get the feel of it."

"Okay."

Fargo realized that if he swung and missed, or got knocked down, the players would probably laugh and he'd have to work even harder to earn their respect. If, however, he hit the ball with any kind of force or authority, he'd probably win it on the spot.

And it still really didn't look that hard to him.

He stepped up to the plate and stood the way he had seen to others stand.

"I'm Leo Gordon," the catcher said.

"Fargo."

"Nice ta meet ya, Fargo," Gordon said. "Better toss that hat away. Might get in your way."

Fargo took the hat off and Flowers was there to hold it for him. He took up his stance again.

Fargo stared out at the pitcher and remembered what Basher had told him—but was he being set up? Did Basher want him to stand his ground so the pitcher *could* hit him with the ball?

The pitcher reared back into what Flowers had told him was called a "windup," and then let the ball go. Fargo kept his eye on it, and he knew that although it was going to come close, it wasn't going to hit him.

He stood his ground. The ball slammed into the leather glove Leo Gordon was wearing with a resounding slap.

"Ball one," the umpire called out.

The catcher threw the ball back to the pitcher, who was glaring at Fargo. Fargo glared back, but he had the feeling he'd already gained a measure of respect by standing in there.

Now, if Basher was right, this one was going to come in straight over the plate.

The pitcher reared back and threw it.

The ball looked huge to Fargo. He was told later that this was what made good hitters. He knew it was coming in straight. He waited . . . waited . . . and then swung. The bat struck the ball with a loud crack. For a moment he thought the bat had broken, and he felt the vibrations from the contact up his hands and wrists, and through his arms.

The ball flew into the air and kept going. All the players turned to watch it. Even the men further out, whose job it was to catch it, simply turned and watched. The ball kept going, and Fargo realized that it was going farther than any other ball he'd seen hit that day.

Everyone was silent. Fargo checked the bat and saw that it wasn't broken.

"Fluke!" the pitcher shouted. "Gimme another ball!"

Somebody tossed another ball out to him.

"You want to try that again?" he demanded of Fargo.

"Sure," Fargo said, emboldened by his success.

The pitcher reached back and threw this one even harder than before.

Crack!

This one went event farther than before, and everyone stood watching in disbelief.

"Again!" the pitcher demanded.

Crack!

Crack!

Crack!

Three more pitches, and three times more the ball went sailing out of sight.

Fargo turned and walked away. He handed Basher the bat, accepted his hat from Flowers along with his gunbelt, which he strapped on.

"That was amazing!" Basher gushed.

"Fargo . . ." Flowers said. "I don't know what to say."

"Maybe I was lucky," Fargo answered.

"Not five times in a row."

Suddenly, Fargo was surrounded by most of the players. For a moment he didn't know what they wanted, but they soon were slapping him on the back, shaking his hand, and introducing themselves. There was no way he'd remember all their names—not yet—but he appreciated the sentiment.

The only player who hadn't approached him was the pitcher, who was still on the mound, still glaring harshly at him.

There was at least one man there Fargo hadn't made friends with.

"Don't mind Catfish."

"Who?" Fargo asked Flowers.

"The pitcher, Catfish Hawkins. His real name is Clem, but everybody calls him Catfish."

They were walking away from the field now, back to town, while the players scattered to pick up their equipment.

"I guess I must have embarrassed him," Fargo said.

"Oh, yeah, I'd say you did."

"I'm real sorry, Mike, but the ball, it just looked so big to me. It was like I couldn't have missed it if I tried."

"Like I said, that's what the great hitters, like Basher, always say," Flowers said. "Fargo—"

"I know what you're going to say."

"You've *got* to play."

"No."

"But you have a natural talent for it."

"No," Fargo repeated. "I don't know the game, Mike. Just from watching, I know there's much more to it than just hitting the ball."

"You can learn the rest," Flowers said, "but hitting . . . you can't really learn that. That's a talent."

"Look, I appreciate the offer, but once we get moving I'll have a lot of other things to do."

"Look," Flowers said, "I have to get back and help collect everything, but think about it, huh?"

Fargo sighed, then said, "Yeah, okay, I'll think about it."

Flowers nodded enthusiastically, slapped him on the back, and ran back to be with his players. Fargo thought that maybe he was going to try to soothe Catfish Hawkins's wounded ego.

8

Fargo was in his hotel room when there was a knock on the door. He had his shirt off and was massaging his lower back. He thought he had probably pulled a muscle swinging that damned baseball bat. It was a movement he was not used to.

He had stopped at the Dutchman's Saloon to tell the Dutchman that he could go over to the general store and buy what he needed to complete his mess.

"I got my own pots and pans," the man had said, "but I do some shopping."

"Tell Mr. Dennis you're working for Mr. Arnold. Okay?" Fargo had replied.

"It's okay!"

Now he walked to the door and opened it, still barechested. There was a young man standing there—little more than a boy, really—looking startled and more than a little scared.

"What can I do for you, son?"

"Uh, are you Mr. Fargo?" His voiced cracked when he said Fargo's name.

"That's right."

"My uncle sent me over," the boy stated.

"And who's your uncle?"

"Uh, my uncle Ralph?"

"Ralph who, boy? I need a little more to go on if I'm going to play this guessing game."

"Oh, uh, sorry," the boy said. "Ralph Dennis. He owns the general store."

"Okay, *now* I know who we're talking about. What's he want?"

"He says the rifles are in, if you want to come and take a look at 'em."

"The Winchesters?"

"Yes, sir."

"Are you the one who went and picked them up?"

"Yes, sir."

"You made good time," Fargo said. "It's barely supper time."

"I know, sir," the boy said, "I'm starved."

"Well, I tell you what, son . . ." Fargo dug into his pockets and came out with four bits. "You have your meal on me."

"Hey, thanks, mister!"

"Enjoy it, and tell your uncle I'll be over there as soon as I can.

"Yes, sir!" the boy said. "He closes soon but he'll stay open and wait for you."

"Okay, well, I'll be right there."

"Thanks again, mister."

"What's your name?"

"Willy."

"Well, you did a good job, Willy. You tell your uncle I said you deserve a bonus."

"Oh, I'll tell 'im," Willy said, "but I doubt that I'll get it."

"Isn't your uncle a fair man to work for?"

"Oh, he's fair," the boy said, nodding, "he's just tight with a dollar, is all."

"I see."

Willy turned to leave, then turned back before Fargo could close the door.

"Can I give you some advice, mister?"

"Sure, Willy," Fargo said. "I can always use some good advice."

"Don't accept my uncle's first offer," Willy said. "He ain't never sold these many rifles at one time before. You can haggle him down some."

"That's real good advice, Willy. You drink beer?"

"Yes, sir," Willy said proudly, then added in a more sheepish tone, "well, I just started."

"Here," Fargo said, and flipped him another two bits. "To wash down that supper with."

"Thanks again!" Willy said, and took off happily down the hall.

Fargo closed the door, put on his shirt, and was out the door seconds later.

When Fargo got to the general store, it was still open for business. The storekeeper, Dennis, waved to him over the head of a customer.

"I'll be right with you, Mr. Fargo."

"No hurry, Mr. Dennis," Fargo said. "Take care of your customer."

The customer was an older lady and she turned and thanked Fargo for his kindness. Fargo just smiled and tipped his hat.

He walked around the door, grabbing an item here and there that he thought they would need for the trip. When the woman finished her business and left, he went up to the counter.

"Sorry to take so long. Mrs. Edgeworth is getting on and it takes her longer to shop these days."

"That's okay. Was the Dutchman in today to buy some supplies?"

"He was here," Dennis said. "Boy and howdy, I've never seen him so happy."

"Did he get what he needed?"

"I think so," Dennis said. "Didn't spend all that much, even though I reminded him a time or two it was Mr. Arnold's money."

"That's good," Fargo said, "it means I can trust him."

"Oh, my, yes," Dennis said, "he's a very trustworthy man. If you'll give me a moment to lock the door, we can go in the back and look at the rifles."

"Fine."

Fargo watched the man lock up, and then he returned to the counter.

"Some extra items for you?"

"Just a few."

Fargo handed them over.

"I'll put them with the other things and add them to Mr. Arnold's bill. If you'll follow me . . ."

Fargo followed Dennis behind the counter and through a doorway into a storage room. There he found a crate of rifles waiting for him.

"The extra ones came in the crate. I put the ones I already had on top."

"I've checked those already," Fargo said. He wondered if Dennis would have mixed the rifles in to try and get a few defective ones by him. He checked the rifles on top carefully—"Can't be too careful," he told Dennis—then got to the new batch.

"These are better than the ones you had," Fargo said, holding one of the rifles.

"Uh, yes, my stock here was older. These are newer weapons."

Fargo checked them all and found them in the same general condition—excellent. He checked the firing mechanism on all the guns and found that they all worked. Of course, the real test would be when they were fired, but he didn't feel the need to take them all out back and test each one.

"All right, Mr. Dennis," Fargo said, "now let's talk price. . . ."

Willy had been right. Fargo had been able to haggle Dennis down from his initial price because of the number of weapons he was buying. While he was at it, Fargo sung his praises of the boy.

"My sister's boy," Dennis said. "I'll make a shop-keeper out of him, yet."

"He tell you what I said?"

"Hmmm? Oh, you mean about a bonus?"

"That's right."

Dennis smiled. "He gets a very good salary, Mr. Fargo," the shopkeeper said. "After all, he is my sis-ter's boy."

"Still," Fargo said pointedly, "I think he deserves a little more."

"Well . . ." Dennis was fidgeting nervously. It was clear that he was afraid of Fargo. "I suppose I can put a little something extra in his pay envelope this week."

"There's a good man," Fargo said. "I'm sure if you asked Mr. Arnold about rewarding your employees, he'd tell you that's how he got where he is today."

"You mean rich?"

"Filthy rich," Fargo corrected. "The man keeps his employees happy, Mr. Dennis. That's why he has a line of credit here."

"Well," Dennis said, "if Mr. Arnold operates that way, I suppose I should too."

Fargo was pleased with the weapons. He wondered, though, if they weren't going to be wasted on this bunch of men. They could catch balls and swing a bat, but how were they going to be at firing rifles?

All Fargo needed now were those extra two men to ride along with them. He'd use them as scouts and flankers, let one of them ride drag for a while. He could probably have used more, but he'd already spoken to Arnold about hiring two. He didn't want to push the man.

When he got back to the hotel, he found Willy waiting for him.

"Hello, Willy."

The boy stood up from the sofa he was sitting on and started fidgeting from foot to foot.

"Can I talk to you, Mr. Fargo?"

"Sure, Willy. What's on your mind?"

"I heard you're puttin' together an expedition to San Francisco."

Fargo wasn't sure he'd call it an expedition, but he said, "That's right."

"I'd like to go with you."

"How old are you, Willy?"

"Nineteen."

"Is that the truth?"

The boy looked down shamedly. "Nineteen next month."

"And why do you want to leave home? What would your parents say?"

"My pa's dead. It's just me and my ma."

"Well then, doesn't she need you here?"

"She needs me to make some money, Mr. Fargo, more than my Uncle Ralph pays me. I only intend to go with you to San Francisco, working my way, and then I'll come back. I heard that Mr. Jack Arnold is a generous employer, and I heard you was lookin' for riders."

"Well, Willy, I was hoping for some experienced riders—"

"I can ride, Mr. Fargo," Willy said, "and I can drive a rig and shoot a rifle. I'm a hard worker."

"I already know you are, Willy."

"Won't you hire me and take me along? Please, sir? I'll work real hard for my wages. I swear I will."

"Willy—"

"I *got* to make some money, Mr. Fargo. I just got to—for my ma."

Fargo frowned at the boy.

"Are you trying to get around me, boy, by using your ma?"

"Well," Willy said, smart enough to exhibit his embarrassment, "maybe just a little."

"You know what, Willy? I like your style. Can your uncle do without you for a while?"

"Oh, sure he can. I don't think he really needs me, anyway. Just pays me a little to keep my ma off his back."

"I see," Fargo said. "Okay, then, you're hired. You'll have to have your own horse and rifle—"

"I got 'em."

"—and I'll need you to see that those supplies your uncle's holding for me get to the livery and onto the wagons for tomorrow."

"I can do that."

"Good. Then I'll see you at first light in front of the livery, Willy."

"By damn!" Willy exclaimed, pounding his fist into his hand. "I really appreciate this, Mr. Fargo."

"Never mind," Fargo said. "Just be ready to go, and be ready to work hard."

"Yes, sir."

"And, Willy?" Fargo caught the boy before he could run from the lobby.

"Yes, sir?"

"You were right about your uncle and those rifles. I'm indebted to you."

"Yes, sir!"

Willy left the hotel and Fargo realized he was going to have to tell Ben Meeker that he only needed one man for the ride, now.

9

"But I've got two men for you," Meeker whined.

Fargo had been afraid this would happen.

"Well, you haven't hired them, have you?"

"I told them I can't hire them, that you have to do that," Meeker said.

"Okay," Fargo said. "I'll interview them and hire one of them."

"They're brothers."

"Is that a problem?"

"You got a brother?"

"No."

"Well, these two are close."

"Then I'll hire someone else."

"These boys are good with their guns, Fargo," Meeker said.

"And trustworthy?"

Meeker didn't answer right away.

"Ben?" Fargo urged.

"If you pay them well enough, I suppose you can trust them."

"Ben—" Fargo's voice had an edge to it now.

"Well, do you know how hard it is to find competent men that you can also trust?"

"No."

"Well, pretty damn hard, especially in this town," Meeker said. "Harder than I thought."

"Maybe I'll make do with the one man," Fargo said. "I can use him to scout the terrain ahead of us."

"Who'd you get?"

"Ralph Dennis's nephew."

"Willy?" Meeker asked incredulously.

"What's wrong with Willy?"

Meeker frowned, took a moment, then said, "Actually, nothing. He's a good boy, a hard worker and, for what you're lookin' for, he'd probably do the trick."

"And can I trust him?"

"Now that I think about it, you could trust Willy more than anybody else in town."

"Well then, I made a good choice. Tell these other fellas that the positions got filled."

"They were kind of lookin' forward to it."

"Who are they?"

"The Benedict brothers," Meeker said.

"Should I know them, Ben?"

"They're known around town," Meeker said, "but no, I don't see any reason why you would have heard of them before now."

"How about my horses?"

"I got some good teams for you," Meeker said. "Want to take a look?"

Fargo knew that Meeker knew horseflesh, but after almost getting stuck with the Benedict brothers he said, "Yeah, might as well."

"Come on over to the livery, then," Meeker said. "I got a jug there, too."

* * *

They walked to the livery and Meeker led the way into his office. He dug out his jug and then said, "Let's go out back and take a look."

They went out the back way to the corral and Fargo took his time going over the teams. They were going to have six wagons, and needed twelve horses to pull them.

"I'll need two extra saddle horses, too, Ben," Fargo decided. "By the way, how's the Ovaro?"

"Great shape," Meeker said. "Fine animal, that one. You know, I could knock some of the price off these other ones if you'd throw him into the deal."

"Nothing doing," Fargo said. "I just need two extra saddle horses."

"I got 'em," Meeker said.

"I assumed you'd make me a good price, anyway, being the fair man you are," Fargo said.

"Let's talk about that in my office," Meeker said.

They went back inside. Meeker hadn't uncorked the jug in all this time, and he did so now.

"Have some?"

"No, thanks."

Meeker took a long swig, shuddered, then corked the jug and put it back.

"Maybe I ain't as fair as you thought, Fargo."

"Why's that, Ben?"

"Well," Meeker said, scratching his head, "everybody's out to make a livin', right?"

"Get to the point, Ben," Fargo said resignedly.

"Arnold's as rich as they come back East, Fargo. And he's lettin' you handle this for him, right?"

"So?"

"So what if we just jack the price up a little bit," Meeker said.

"No."

"Don't you want to even think about it?"

"No," Fargo said, "and I'm starting to think maybe I was wrong about you, Ben, for even asking me that."

"Hey," Meeker said, putting up his hands, "forget I said anything, okay? It was just a thought."

Fargo remained quiet.

"I got the price written right down here, Fargo," Meeker said, retrieving a bill from his desk. "And I tell you what. Because I insulted you, I'll throw in them two saddle horses. Whataya say?"

"I'll take the bill to Mr. Arnold," Fargo said, accepting the piece of paper. "He'll pay you before he leaves town."

"I know he will," Meeker said. "He's good for the money."

Fargo turned to leave.

"Hey, Fargo . . ."

Fargo turned.

"Gimme a break, huh?" Meeker said. "It was just a thought, ya know? I'm tryin' to make a buck here."

"Let's just forget it ever happened, Ben."

"Okay," Meeker said, "fine, it's forgotten. It never came up. Can I buy you a drink at the Dutchman's?"

"Maybe later," Fargo said. "I'll see you over there."

"Okay, sure thing," Meeker replied. "Nice doin' business with you, Fargo."

"Sure, Ben," Fargo said, "real nice."

As Fargo went out the door, he was thinking about what he got for being such an honest, trustworthy sort himself. He just expected other people to be that way, too, sometimes—not often, but sometimes—they were. Ben Meeker had seemed decent to him for the first four days he was in Kansas City, but as soon as they were in a position to do business together . . .

Well, it just went to show you, Fargo thought, *never do business with a friend—especially a brand-new friend you really don't know all that well.*

Fargo had definitely been in Kansas City too long.

Fargo stopped at the Dutchman's and had a beer and struck up a conversation with the Dutchman himself, who was obviously ready to go.

"What are you going to do about your place while you're gone?" Fargo asked.

"I have someone to run it," the Dutchman said.

"Look," Fargo said, "we can't just keep calling you 'the Dutchman' during the whole trip. You must have a name . . . don't you?"

"I have a name you cannot say," the Dutchman replied, which Fargo took to mean he wouldn't be able to pronounce. "How about you call me Dutch?"

"Dutch it is," Fargo said. "That's easy enough to remember, and to say."

"And you are Fargo."

"Right," Fargo said, "Skye Fargo."

"Sky?" Dutch asked, pointing up.

"That's right."

"Dat is a nice name, Sky."

"Thanks."

"Sky . . ." Dutch said again, nodding and smiling. "Nice name."

At that point, the batwings opened and Meeker came walking in, looking harried. When he saw Fargo, he hurried to the bar. Fargo frowned, not happy to see the man so soon after their business.

"I'm having a quiet drink, Ben," Fargo said.

"I can see that. I just wanted to warn you."

"About what?"

"The boys."

"What boys?"

"The Benedict boys."

"The trustworthy men you wanted me to hire?" Fargo asked. "What about them?"

"Well . . . when I told them the job wasn't theirs, they sort of, uh, didn't take it too well."

"So? That's your problem."

"Well . . . it's really your problem."

"And why's that?"

"Because you were the one doing the hiring," he said. "I told them you didn't want them to tag along."

"You phrased it that way?"

"Well . . . yeah, how was I supposed to phrase it?" Meeker asked.

"Well, it would have been nice if you'd simply told them that I hired someone else."

Meeker frowned and asked, "What's the difference?"

"The difference," Fargo said, "is that maybe they wouldn't be so riled right now."

Meeker shrugged, apparently still not seeing the difference.

"It doesn't matter," Fargo said. "Just keep them away from me."

"Well, that ain't gonna be too easy."

"Why not?"

"They're kinda lookin' for you right now."

Fargo turned toward Meeker.

"Now, don't get mad at me . . ." Meeker said.

"Who should I get mad at, Ben?"

"I thought we was friends."

"I thought so, too, until a little while ago," Fargo replied. "Now, I'm thinking I made a mistake. I make friends too fast."

"Aw, now . . ." Meeker retorted, wincing as if in pain. "I thought we settled that—"

"Ben," Fargo interrupted, "you better tell those boys to stay away from me, because if I have to tangle with them, you're going to tangle with me."

"Fargo—"

"Am I making myself clear enough?"

Meeker scowled and said, "Sure."

"Good," Fargo said. "Now I'm going to finish my beer."

"How am I supposed to keep them away from you?"

"That's your problem."

Meeker bit his lip, then snapped his fingers, and headed for the batwing doors, muttering something that sounded like "Sheriff."

10

Fargo was truly angry about the situation with the Benedicts, which he felt Meeker had caused. He didn't want to end up having to fight with them, hurting them—or worse. Fargo himself didn't want to get hurt either—or worse.

He had several choices that he could see. He could stay indoors, either in his hotel or at the Dutchman's. Neither of those choices appealed to him. He could simply go about his business and see if and when the Benedicts caught up him. At that time, maybe he'd be able to explain things to them.

Or he could go to the sheriff, which was what Meeker seemed to have in mind.

"Dutch?"

"Ya?"

"Do you know the Benedict brothers?"

"Ya, I know," Dutch said in a disgusted tone, leaning his big elbows on the bar. "Bad boys."

"How bad?"

"They like to hurt people."

"Killers?"

Dutch thought a moment, then said, "I don't tink . . . but dey are young. They could learn."

"What are we talking about here, men or boys?"

"Young men," Dutch said, "twenty, maybe, the other twenty-two or -three."

"You know their names?"

"Dirk and Dack."

"Really?"

Dutch nodded.

"Parents didn't have much imagination, did they?"

"Dere father's name was Dick."

"I see. I wonder what the mother's name was . . . no, never mind. I don't want to know them that well."

"Dey take one look at you," Dutch said, "and you have no trouble from dem boys."

"I hope not," Fargo replied. "I've got one more night here and I don't need trouble."

"I tink maybe trouble follows you, no?"

Fargo scowled himself, now, and said, "Sometimes I think you're right."

"You stay here," Dutch said. "I have shotgun behind bar. You have no trouble."

"That's the problem, Dutch," Fargo said. "I don't want to feel like I'm hiding."

"You not hiding," Dutch said, "you . . . what is it . . . ah, you avoiding."

"Still feels like hiding to me," Fargo said. "Sometimes I wish I was one of them fellas that have no ego at all."

"Ego not a bad thing."

"Sometimes it is," Fargo said. "Sometimes it gets you killed."

"But not you."

"No," Fargo said, "not yet." Fargo knocked superstitiously on the bar with his knuckles and said, "I'll see you a little later, Dutch."

"You come back later?"

"Yep, I'll come back later."

"You come back, I buy you a beer."

"It's a deal."

Fargo turned and strode out the batwing doors.

Fargo checked off a list in his head while he walked down the street. By the time he reached his hotel, he thought that they had done everything that needed to be done. All they needed to do was meet at the livery in the morning. He kept walking past the hotel and continued to the rooming house where Mike Flowers and the team were staying.

This time when he knocked at the door, it was answered by a woman in her early fifties—but an attractive woman who wore the years well. She was tall, angular, her body toned from years of hard work. Her hands were the only part of her that seemed aged.

"Well, handsome," she said, leaning against the wall, "if I thought you were here lookin' for me, I'd die a happy woman tomorrow."

"Ma'am," Fargo said, removing his hat and smiling, "if I only had the time."

"Liar!" she said, but she was smiling too. "What can I do for you?"

"I'm looking for a man named Mike Flowers."

"Flowers," she said, laughing. "Ain't that a helluva name?"

"We can't all pick our names, ma'am."

"Ain't that the truth," she said. "I picked my man and I ended up bein' Mrs. Sunderly—now the widow Sunderly. And my first name ain't much better."

"What is it?"

"Gertrude."

He saw what she meant.

"Ain't much you can do with that beyond Gert, and that ain't much better," she said.

"Is Flowers in, ma'am?"

"Damned if I know," she said. "Some of them others are here, that whatayacallit, baseball team?"

"Yes, ma'am."

"Have you ever seen that game?"

"Saw some just this morning."

"Stupidest damned thing I ever saw."

"It did seem kind of silly."

"Well, you wanna come in and ask some of them if they seen him? They're sitting around my parlor."

"Thank you, ma'am, I think I will."

"Come ahead, then."

She backed away so he could enter and she led him to the parlor.

"Hey, look who it is! Our new hitter!"

Fargo located the one of the five men who was speaking, and saw that it was Basher.

"Hello, Basher."

"Man, you gave that ball a lift," Basher said, approaching him and sticking out his hand. This time he was so enthusiastic he almost did crush Fargo's hand. "Where'd you get off to today? I wanted to talk to you some more."

"I had some things to do."

"He's too good to associate with the likes of us," another man said.

Fargo looked over and recognized the man whose pitches he had hit so far. He'd forgotten his name. He remembered, though, that Basher's real name was Vince Hogan. He also recognized the "catcher," Leo Gordon.

"That ain't it at all, friend," Fargo said. "There's a lot to be done if we're going to leave for San Francisco in the morning."

"Oh, that's right," the man said with a sneer in his voice, "you're our native guide, ain't you?"

"Lay off of him, Catfish," Gordon said.

Now he remembered. Catfish Hawkins.

"Don't tell me what to do, Gordon," Hawkins said angrily. "If you'd called for better pitches, maybe he wouldn't have hit them."

Basher laughed. "Hell, Catfish, you was throwin' your best stuff and he still whaled the tar out of it."

"Better than you could ever do, Basher."

The big man still laughed.

"Any time you want to try throwin' it by me, Catfish, I'm ready." Basher turned and looked at Fargo. "You lookin' for the skipper?"

It took Fargo a minute to realize he was referring to Flowers.

"That's right."

"He ain't around right now. Said he had to go into town to buy something."

"Maybe I'll run into him there, then," Fargo said. "If I don't, just tell him we're all set to leave tomorrow. You boys have to be at the livery early, just after first light."

"We'll be there," Basher said. "And don't mind nothin' Catfish says. He's just embarrassed 'cause you hit his best stuff."

"I wasn't trying to embarrass anyone," Fargo said. "I thought it was just a game."

"It is," Basher said, and then added, "to some people."

11

Fargo had met the sheriff of Kansas City the first day in town. His name was Creed, and he'd been the star-packer in the town for about six years. He came by the hotel when he heard Fargo was in town just to have a "little chat." He hadn't seen the man since. This led Fargo to believe the man was good at his job. He'd checked him out when he arrived, found out his business, and then left him alone.

Now, as Fargo walked back toward the center of town from Mrs. Sunderly's house, Sheriff Frank Creed was coming toward him.

"Sheriff," Fargo said with a nod.

"Mr. Fargo."

They stopped right in the center of the board-walk, then moved aside in concert so people could continue on without being blocked.

"I understand you'll be leavin' us tomorrow."

"That's right," Fargo confirmed. "Got a job taking some people to San Francisco."

"Those baseball people, I heard."

"You heard right."

"Also heard somethin' else."

"And what might that be, Sheriff?"

"That you might be havin' some trouble with the Benedict brothers."

"I don't know," Fargo said. "Maybe you can tell me if I might."

Creed was about fifty, starting to show a paunch above his gunbelt, and some gray beneath his hat. He had a mustache that hid his mouth—the upper lip, anyway—and it had gone gray a long time ago.

"They're hotheaded boys, Fargo," Creed said, "but probably nothing a man like you would have to worry about."

"What kind of man is that, Sheriff?"

"Experienced," the lawman said. "You got a lot more experience than them, and you've also had it with worse than them."

"What is it you're telling me, Sheriff?"

"I guess what I'm askin' is that if they do brace you, I'd appreciate it if you didn't kill 'em."

"Well, no, that's not something I'd be looking forward to doing."

"That's good to hear."

"But I'm not about to let them kill me, either."

"No, I wouldn't expect that."

"Now tell me something."

"What's that?"

"Are you going to have the same conversation with them that you're having with me?"

"I sure am," he said, then added, "as soon as I find them."

Fargo found Jack Arnold that night at the same place he'd found him that first time, the night before—in the Silver Spur Saloon. Once again, he was surrounded by men with pads and pencils, waiting for pearls of wisdom to come flowing out of his mouth.

"Gentlemen," he said, as Fargo approached, "I'll have to ask you to excuse me now. Business calls."

The reporters reluctantly stood up and moved away, but they didn't go far. They lined up at the bar, where they continued to drink on Jack Arnold's tab.

"Have a seat, Mr. Fargo," Arnold said. "Tell me where we stand."

"It's just Fargo, Mr. Arnold," Fargo said, sitting across from the man.

"That's fine," Arnold said. "How do we look, Fargo?"

"We'll be leaving in the morning," Fargo stated. "Everything is arranged."

"You found your two men, then?"

Fargo was about to say no, but then he realized that he had, indeed, hired two men—the boy, Willy, and the big Dutchman.

"Yes, I did."

"And you have everything else you need?"

"Wagons, horses, supplies, and rifles."

"A rifle for each man?"

"That's right."

"Must have been expensive."

"I got you a good price."

"Did you, now?" Arnold asked. "Well, that's good news, Fargo, real good news. Why don't you have a beer while you're here?"

"Don't mind if I do."

Arnold waved, and it was obvious he had the bartender trained because the man immediately appeared with two beers.

"Thank you, Cecil."

"My pleasure, Mr. Arnold."

Fargo picked up the beer and sipped it. The beer at the Dutchman's was colder, and cheaper.

"I heard you embarrassed my star pitcher this morning," Arnold said.

"It wasn't something I was trying to do."

"I also heard you hit the ball real well. I had a feeling about you the first time I saw you."

"I remember."

"You have played before, haven't you?"

"Never."

"And you hit the ball that well?"

"I got lucky."

"Five times?"

"You have all your facts straight, don't you?" Fargo asked.

"I always do. Tell me, how were you able to hit so well?"

"It just didn't look that hard to do."

"And I guess it wasn't."

Fargo shrugged.

"Well," Arnold said, "if you're so bound and determined not to play for my team, I'd appreciate it if you would refrain from showing any more of them up."

"That's something I can promise you, Mr. Arnold."

"Good, very good," Arnold said. "Then I guess the next time we see each other will be in San Francisco."

"I guess so."

"And all my players will be there," Arnold added, "safe and sound?"

Fargo finished his beer and stood up.

"They will if they do everything I tell them to do on the way."

"That's something I can promise you, Fargo."

"Even your star pitcher?"

Arnold thought a moment, then said, "I'll have a word with him."

"Fine."

"Of course," Arnold said, "if you'd consider stepping up to bat against him again, and this time you struck out five times—"

"That wouldn't be showing him very much respect, would it, Mr. Arnold . . . or me."

"I suppose not."

"Anyway," Fargo continued, "I'd be just as happy never to pick one of those bats up again."

"Have it your way, Fargo."

"I usually do, Mr. Arnold."

"You should have stayed around last night when I invited you," Arnold said. "Miss Benet came over and sat with me for a while, and then she and I . . . well, a gentleman shouldn't tell, but she and I went back to my room."

"Did you?"

"Oh, yes," Arnold said. "Didn't you know? Women love men with money. They'll do almost anything for it—and Miss Benet was no exception." Arnold's smile was ugly. "She . . . did . . . everything."

The leer on Arnold's face was something Fargo wanted to erase. He knew Arnold was lying. What Arnold didn't know was that Fargo knew it, and why.

"I'll probably end up with her in my room again tonight," the wealthy man said.

"Is that a fact?"

"Well, I don't know, for sure," Arnold said. "I'll let you know tomorrow."

"By the time you wake up tomorrow," Fargo said, "I'll be gone."

"Oh, that's right," Arnold said. "Well then, I suppose you'd better just wish me luck, then."

This time, Fargo returned Arnold's ugly smile.

"You'll need all the luck you can get, Arnold."

Jack Arnold frowned, as if he wasn't sure what Fargo meant by that, but he didn't pursue the matter further.

"Oh, by the way," he said, before Fargo could leave, "another member of my team arrived in town today and will be accompanying you on the trip to San Francisco."

"I've got everything set up for twenty-six men," Fargo said.

"There won't be a problem," Arnold said. "Flowers will introduce the two of you tomorrow morning."

"Suit yourself," Fargo said, "it's your team."

"I usually do," Arnold said.

As he left, the reporters detached themselves from the bar and once again descended upon the wealthy businessman from the East.

Fargo left the saloon annoyed, and what happened next annoyed him even more.

"Hey!" he heard a voice call.

He turned and saw two men approaching him from across the street. It was getting dark, so he had to wait until they were almost on him to be able to see their faces. They looked enough alike to be brothers.

The Benedict brothers.

"You Fargo?" one of them asked.

"That's right."

"I'm Dirk Benedict," the speaker said, "and this is my brother Dack."

"What can I do for you boys?"

"We had jobs with you, mister," Dack said, "and you took 'em away."

"I never gave you boys jobs," Fargo said. "You talked to Ben Meeker."

"He said you'd hire us."

"He was wrong."

Fargo turned to walk away.

"Don't turn your back on us, mister!" Dack Benedict called out. "It ain't polite."

Fargo turned back. He didn't know which one had said that, because they not only looked alike, they sounded alike, as well.

"If you boys are looking for trouble, I'd advise you to look someplace else."

"Hey, mister," Dirk said, "all we want is an explanation."

"How come we didn't get those jobs?" Dack added.

Would it be this easy? Just explain it to them and they'd let it go?

"Okay," Fargo said, turning to face them square on. "Before Meeker got to me with your names, I hired another man. That's all there was to it."

The two brothers exchanged a glance. Both were wearing guns, and Fargo noted with curiosity that one of them had his gun on his left hip, and the other on the right.

"Is that good enough for you boys?"

The two of them exchanged a glance, and then one said, "No. You owe us jobs, mister. You're cheatin' us—"

"Look, fellas—"

Suddenly, one of them unbuckled his gunbelt, and then the other did the same. Both guns fell to the ground.

"We got to whup you."

"What?"

"You cheated us, and we got to whup you."

He couldn't even tell if the same man had spoken or if they'd taken turns. He knew if he shot them now he'd be shooting unarmed men. He either had to fight, or turn and run—and there was just no run in Skye Fargo.

He didn't have time to think anymore. One of the brothers rushed him, bulling him into a hitching post. Fargo's attacker tried to get his arms around him, to pin his arms to his side, but Fargo head-butted the man, opening a gash on the man's head. He stepped back, releasing Fargo, who then stepped forward and hit the man with his right fist. The bleeding man went down like he was poleaxed.

The other brother had been frozen all this time, but now he roared and charged Fargo—but the Trailsman had seen that move once before. He side-stepped and let the man's charge take him past him, into the hitching post, and this time it gave from the impact. Both man and post went to the dirt, and then the man slowly got up.

"Back off, son," Fargo said, but Benedict—Dack

78

or Dirk, he couldn't tell which—swung a right at Fargo. He ducked under it, hit the younger man in the belly with two quick punches, taking the air out of him, and then finished him with the same right that finished his brother.

He walked away, leaving both men lying on the ground.

12

"He what?"

"He told me you went to his room with him last night and had a good time."

Brenda Benet sat straight up in bed, giving Fargo a clear look at her smooth, beautiful back. He loved the way the line down the center of her back disappeared between her buttocks. *A woman's back just might be the most beautiful thing in the world*, he thought. He put his hand out and stroked it, and felt the tension that coursed through her.

"That pig!" she shouted. "I hope you called him a liar."

"Nope."

"Punched him?"

"No."

She looked at him over her shoulder.

"Why not?"

"I thought you'd like to be the one to do those things," he said.

She half turned to face him, her hair falling down to cover her face.

"You know," she said, "you're right. I *would* like to do it."

"I know."

"Would you like to be there to see it?"

"I'd love to," he said, "but by that time I'll be gone, heading for San Francisco."

She pouted. "I forgot all about that."

"I didn't," he said. "Come here."

He gathered her into his arms and kissed her deeply, turning her so that she was lying on her back. He kissed her lips, then her chin, then her neck, then her breasts, lingering over each nipple for a while until she squirmed, and then he continued down again. His journey took him over her ribs to her belly, where he paused to lick her navel, and then further down again. He kissed her hips, rolled her over slightly so he could kiss her buttocks, then moved to her thighs and legs, worked his way down one leg, kissed her ankle and the toes, then back up the other one, lingering behind her knee.

"Ooooh, God, I'm so relaxed I can't believe it." She moaned. "Oh, you do that so good."

He continued up her leg with his mouth but moved one hand between her thighs and began to stroke her bush gently.

"Oh, Skye, yes . . . you're so gentle it's unbelievable . . ."

His stroking fingers made her wet by the time his mouth got there. He licked her gently, just on the surface, then delved between the folds of flesh for more.

She squeezed her eyes shut and wiggled her hips as his licking became more insistent. He slid his hands beneath her to cup her buttocks and lift her so he could have better access to her. He used his tongue to lick the entire length of her wet slit.

He was enjoying every minute of it, enjoying the

taste and smell of her, and then he worked on her until he felt her body tremble, felt the rush of sensations tumble through her until she cried out and began to gasp and flop around on the bed as he held her.

"Oh, God, don't . . . you're killing me . . . let me . . . go . . . no, don't . . . I can't take . . . any . . . more . . ."

Suddenly, she went limp, as if she'd passed out, and he chose that moment to mount her and slide into her.

"Oh, God!" she gasped, her eyes opening wide.

As he began to move above her, she laughed and cried and clutched at him. His strokes became longer and harder until he no longer heard the sounds she was making because he was grunting and groaning so hard as he strained for his own release . . . and found it.

"It's probably good that you're leaving in the morning," she said.

"Why's that?"

"Any more nights like this," she said, "and one of us would have a heart attack for sure."

He laughed, stroked her hip and said, "This night isn't over, yet."

Fargo woke the next morning before the first light. Brenda had stayed with him in his room and he had to slide his left arm out from beneath her without waking her so he could get up and dress.

They had decided not to say good-bye. She insisted that when he rose in the morning, he should leave without waking her, if he could. They would meet again, she said, she was sure of it, probably in San Francisco.

"It's fate," she had said, "and I believe in fate."

So he dressed quietly, picked up his saddlebags and rifle, and left the room without waking her.

He hoped.

When he got to the livery, he thought he was the first one to arrive. Meeker had the teams hitched to the wagons and they were all out in front of the stable.

"Morning," Meeker said, from the back of one of the wagons.

"Good morning."

"Thought I'd make up for my foolish behavior by helping you get ready."

"I appreciate that, Ben."

That was when he found out he really hadn't arrived first. The boy, Willy, came out of the livery and said, "Good mornin', Mr. Fargo."

"Morning, Willy—and it's just Fargo."

"Yes, sir," Willy said. "I got the supplies in the back of the first wagon."

The first three wagons were covered Conestogas, the last three were open wagons, more buckboards than anything else. Most of the men and supplies would ride in the first three. He didn't want to overtax the last three. If they'd had more time, he would have waited for three better wagons, but they didn't. They'd have to make do.

"That's good, Willy."

"Wanna see?"

"Yeah, I'll take a look."

"Want me to saddle the Ovaro?" Meeker asked.

"I'll take care of it, Ben," Fargo said. "Thanks."

He found the man's contrite behavior even more annoying than anything else. Suddenly, he couldn't wait to be away from Kansas City.

He walked with Willy to the front wagon and took a look. The supplies had been equally distributed throughout the wagon.

"Looks like you know what you're doing," Fargo complimented him.

"If I didn't learn nothing' else from my uncle, I learned how to load supplies onto a wagon."

"I can see that," Fargo said. He clapped the boy on the shoulder and said, "I guess I made the right choice, didn't I?"

Willy beamed.

"Where are the rifles?"

"In there, underneath those sacks," Willy said. "I thought they'd better not be in plain sight."

"It was a good thought, Willy, but they have to be accessible so we can get to them."

Willy looked crestfallen.

"I didn't think of that. I was thinking—you know—about Indians, and stuff."

"Don't worry," Fargo said. "Just shift some of those sacks so we can get to the guns quickly if we have to."

Not that he knew, yet, who could shoot and who couldn't. He'd have to use part of the first day to find out who could hit what he aimed at, and who was more likely to shoot himself in the foot.

"Where's your horse?" Fargo asked.

"Inside, saddled and ready."

"I better go saddle mine, then," Fargo said. "The rest should be arriving any time, now."

While he was saddling his Ovaro, he heard the

voices from outside that signaled the arrival of the other twenty-six men, apparently all at once. When he walked the Ovaro outside, they were all milling around. Suddenly, he became aware of a particular voice which sounded odd among the others.

The voice of a woman.

A couple of them greeted him with "Good mornings"—Basher, and Leo Gordon, and the manager, Mike Flowers, approached him.

"I thought we'd wait for you before we started piling into the wagons. You'll probably want to distribute the men."

"Do I hear a woman?" Fargo asked.

"Oh, that's right," Flowers said, "you haven't met Bri."

"Who?"

"Bri," Flowers said, then turned and called the name out louder. "Bri!"

"Yes?"

The woman appeared, tall and willowy, about twenty-five, wearing men's jeans and shirt, a pair of boots, and an amused look on her pretty face.

"Fargo, this is Bridget Arnold."

"Arnold?" Fargo repeated.

"That's right," Flowers said. "Jack's daughter."

"I'll be representing my father on this trip, Mr. Fargo," she said, sticking out her hand. "It's a pleasure to meet you."

Fargo shook her hand, but kept looking at Flowers.

"Nice to meet you, too, Miss Arnold."

"Please, call me Bridget," she said, "or Bri, like everyone else does."

"All right, Bri. Can you excuse us for a minute? I have to talk to Mike about something."

"Sure," she said, still looking amused.

Fargo grabbed Flowers by the arm and pulled him into the stable.

"Are you crazy?" he asked. "Is Arnold crazy? A woman? His daughter? On a trip like this with twenty-six men?"

"Twenty-nine," Flowers said, "you forgot you and Willy—"

"Never mind!" Fargo said. "This has all the earmarks of trouble, Mike."

"Not at all, Fargo," Flowers replied. "Remember, she's Jack's daughter. The whole team knows that, and knows her. They treat her like one of the boys. You'll see."

"Where is she going to ride? And sleep? I mean—"

"She'll ride and sleep where everyone else does, and take her turn doing . . . well, whatever we're going to be doing. Believe me, she'll pull her weight . . . and she's right about one thing."

"What's that?"

"She will be Jack's representative on the trip. Why not let her worry about everything?"

"You're right," Fargo said resignedly after a moment's hesitation. "All right then. Let's get started."

They went back outside.

"All settled?" Bri asked.

Fargo smiled and said, "Everything's fine." He raised his voice and called out, "Which of you can drive?"

Eight men raised their hands, which was better than he'd hoped for. Six would have to drive, and two would be alternates.

"Come with me," Fargo said.

He took the eight men to the wagons and assigned one to each, and the two alternates to the first two. Then he told Flowers how he wanted the men distributed in the six wagons so that most of the weight was carried by the first three. While he was doing that, Dutch arrived, carrying his pots and pans, making enough of a racket to wake the dead.

"Which is my chuck wagon?" he asked.

"We don't have a chuck wagon, Dutch, but we'll do the best we can," Fargo said. "Most of the supplies are in the first wagon. That's where you'll ride."

"Yah," he said, "the first wagon is good."

Some of the players had obviously broken their manager's curfew at some time while they were in town, because they knew the bartender, and he knew them.

Flowers saw the look on Fargo's face, and he shrugged and said, "I can't tie them down. I do the best I can."

Fargo nodded, as if to indicate that was all the man could do.

It was noisy now, with men yelling and laughing and pots and pans clanging together. They were piling into the wagons, though, and by the time the sun was starting to peek out, they were ready to go.

Fargo mounted the Ovaro and rode up and down the length of the six wagons.

"Okay, quiet down!" he called out. "We're waking the whole town."

It took a few minutes, but eventually they all fell silent.

"We're not going to cover very much ground the first day," Fargo said.

"Why not?" Catfish Hawkins asked.

"Because we don't know each other," Fargo said, "and you men don't know the wagons. We'll use the first day to get used to each other."

"It'll take longer than that," Hawkins said, and some of the men laughed.

"For some, maybe," Fargo said. "We have a long way to go, and we're only going to get there if we cooperate."

"You mean if we listen to you, don't you?" Hawkins asked.

"Quiet down and let the man talk, Catfish!" Basher yelled out.

"He's right," Fargo said, "I do expect you all to listen to me. We're going to be in country that I know and you don't. That makes it in your best interest to do everything I say."

"He's got a point there," Leo Gordon said. "He's callin' the signs."

Fargo assumed that was baseball catcher talk, and it sounded right.

"If we've got that straight—Willy, you mounted?"

"Yessir!"

"Okay, then," Fargo said, "let's move out."

13

As expected, they didn't cover much ground the first day. A couple of the men had trouble with their teams and it turned out they had never driven a wagon over this kind of terrain before. They kept getting stuck, having to be pushed or pulled out. Fargo was determined to give some driving lessons the next day.

That night they camped, circling the wagons for safety, and Fargo broke out the rifles while Dutch was preparing their food. He took the men outside the circle of the wagons to practice. Willy, who already knew how to shoot, stood watch.

"All right," Fargo said, "who says they can shoot?"

"Me."

He turned and saw Catfish Hawkins.

"I can pitch," the man said, "and shoot."

Fargo handed him one of the six rifles he'd taken out for practice.

"How about that tree, about twenty yards away?" he asked.

"What part of it?" Hawkins asked.

"Dead center, the trunk."

"How about that sapling next to it?" the pitcher asked.

"That's kind of a small target," Fargo said, "but go ahead."

Hawkins shouldered the weapon, sighted briefly, and fired, cutting the sapling in half.

"Well," Fargo said, impressed, "the man can shoot."

"I said I could," he replied. "I grew up hunting jackrabbits. If you can hit a jack on the run, you can hit anything."

"Obviously," Fargo said.

Hawkins tried to hand the rifle back.

"Hold on to it," Fargo said. "It's one of the better ones."

Hawkins nodded, but said nothing.

"Do me a favor," Fargo said.

"What's that?"

"Just stand over there, across from Willy, and keep watch."

"Sure thing."

Hawkins started to walk away, then turned back.

"What?" Fargo asked.

"Why doesn't the boy have to practice?" he asked.

Fargo was about to answer when Willy said, "I'll shoot." He stepped up. "It's only fair."

"Just hit the tree, Willy," Fargo said. "That's all that's required."

"There's a branch, a broken one hanging down. See it?" Willy asked.

"I see it," said Fargo.

Willy shouldered his rifle and fired, and the

branch wasn't hanging down anymore. He lowered the rifle and exchanged a look with Hawkins.

"Good shooting, Willy," Fargo said. "Next!"

"What about me?" Bridget Arnold asked.

Fargo turned and looked at her, then at Mike Flowers, who was standing behind her.

"Fine," Fargo said, "take your turn."

She approached and he handed her a rifle.

"Willy left a piece of branch on that tree," she said. "I'll take it off."

Before Fargo could respond, she shouldered the rifle and fired in one quick motion. The rest of the branch leaped off the tree. She turned and gave Fargo the rifle, with her patented amused look.

"I've won contests at carnivals and turkey shoots back home."

"Impressive," Fargo said nonchalantly, and dropped it. Her amused look faded. Apparently, she wanted to hear him praise her more than that.

"Next!" he called, again.

Out of the twenty-six men, five were able to hit the tree on the second or third shot. Three, not counting Hawkins, scored on the first shot. And, of course, there was Bri. Six of them hit the tree on the fourth, fifth or sixth shot. The rest of them never hit it at all. These were the eleven who would probably shoot themselves if Fargo gave them a rifle.

"We'll practice each night when we stop," he said when they were finished, "everyone but you eleven men."

"Why not us?" Leo Gordon complained.

"Because you're too dangerous to ever give a rifle to again," Fargo said good-naturedly. "You men will gather wood for the fire, get water, help Dutch, take care of the horses, and whatever else needs doing."

The eleven of them grumbled.

"Everybody's got to pull their weight," Fargo reminded them.

"And everybody's got to practice baseball," Mike Flowers added, "or have you all forgotten why we're here?"

Flowers then looked at Fargo. "We'll have to work something out so that we can get our practice in each night," he said.

"We can do that," Fargo said.

"Chow time!" Dutch shouted.

"Let's do it over supper," Fargo said, and they all returned to the circle of wagons for food.

After they ate, Fargo set the watch. He picked five men to rotate duty, including Willy and Hawkins. At the last minute he threw Bri in, since she was one of the better shots. She didn't complain.

"What are we watching for?" Hawkins asked.

"Anything," Fargo told him. "Indians, bandits, cougars, clouds of dust . . . anything you're not sure about, I want to know about."

"What are you so worried about?" Hawkins asked.

"Out here, Hawkins," Fargo said, "there are too many things to worry about to be able to count them. Just keep your eyes open."

Hawkins made a disgusted grunting sound, but said nothing else.

Fargo returned to the fire and allowed Dutch to fill his coffee cup. He drank coffee while the men who weren't on watch practiced fielding with their bare hands.

Dutch came up alongside him.

"Good food, Dutch." The bartender had prepared a great meaty stew.

"I told you I could cook."

Together they watched the men throwing a ball back and forth between them.

"I am surprised about the woman here," Dutch said, and Fargo nodded, the thought weighing heavily on his own mind all evening.

"So was I."

"One woman, all dese men," Dutch said. "Trouble."

"I've been assured not," Fargo replied. "After all, she's the boss's daughter."

Dutch shook his head and said again, "Trouble."

They watched the practice a little longer and then Dutch said, "Dis does not seem to be something for grown men to do," and walked away.

Fargo thought he might have a point.

After breakfast the next morning, they broke camp. Before turning in the night before, Fargo had talked to the men who'd had trouble handling the western teams. It turned out that both of their experiences had been with driving milk wagons back East.

This, they were finding out, was very different.

When they camped the next night, Flowers came and ate by Fargo. Bri, who had eaten with the men before them, came over and asked if she could join them. Both men said of course, she could.

"What's the first town we'll come to?" Flowers asked.

"Depends on what you want to do. We've already bypassed Topeka."

"Topeka. That's a pretty big town, ain't it?" Flowers asked.

"Yes, it is."

"Why did we bypass it?" Bri asked.

"We don't need any supplies."

"Fargo," Bri said, "we're supposed to be putting on exhibitions along the way. We have to stop at towns like that."

Fargo looked at Flowers, who nodded and said, "She has a point."

"Now you tell me," Fargo said. "If you keep stopping at towns along the way to play baseball, we'll never get to San Francisco."

"And if we don't play games," Flowers said, "then we came all this way for nothing."

Fargo shook his head.

"This trip is going to cost your boss a little more than we agreed on," he said. "I didn't expect to be out here for months."

"Well," Bri said, "we don't want to take *months* to get there. There must be some kind of middle ground."

Both men sat and ate in silence for a few moments.

"It doesn't do you any good to play in small towns, does it?" Fargo finally asked.

"No, none," Flowers said. "We need to play in towns that have a newspaper that will write about it."

"Okay," Fargo said, "at least that gives me some

idea of what you want to do. We probably won't stop anywhere until we cross the border in Colorado. Colorado Springs seems a likely place."

"I've heard of it," Flowers said, enthused. "That seems like a good place to stop to me."

"Okay, then," Fargo said, "we've agreed."

They worked out a schedule whereby Fargo could work with some of the men on their shooting while Flowers held practice with the others, and then they'd switch. This was the routine for the next few days of the trip.

They also worked out a good system for the men whose jobs it was to do the menial tasks, and for the men who were to stand watch. By the end of the first week, they weren't having any trouble with driving the wagons, making or breaking camp, or standing watch. Bri was carrying her weight, as promised, but no longer looked so amused when she and Fargo encountered each other.

For his own part, Fargo started to notice things about her. She had some freckles on the bridge of her nose, her breasts were small, like peaches, but they looked firm. Her legs seemed impossibly long.

He also realized that he didn't care that she was the boss's daughter.

"This is working out okay," Flowers said to Fargo one night over supper. "This bartender sure can cook."

"That's a pleasant surprise on a trip like this," Fargo said. "Any time you find someone who can cook for a bunch of men, you've got yourself a gem."

"The men are holding up well, too," Flowers noted. "I thought a trip like this might break them down some, but they're getting used to the chores you've given them."

"Most of them are."

"Bri?"

"No," Fargo said. He looked across the camp at where she was eating with some of the men, laughing and talking among them. She looked over at Fargo. Then averted her eyes when she saw him looking at her. "She's okay."

"Still having trouble with Hawkins?" Flowers asked.

"Nothing I can't handle," Fargo said. "There's a defiant streak in him, but he can shoot, and he's got good eyes when he's on watch."

"Like calling you because he saw a jackrabbit?"

Fargo laughed.

"He wanted to see which one of us could shoot it first."

"And who did?"

"Neither," Fargo said. "I don't kill for sport, and we have plenty of food. We didn't need it to eat. He doesn't call me for stuff like that anymore."

"Hawkins is a good kid, really," Flowers said. "So's the boy, Willy."

"I know it," Fargo said. "He's a good worker."

"He's real interested in baseball, too."

"Is he?"

"Yep. Keeps asking me if he can practice with the team one night. What do you think?"

"It's your team. Think he can play?"

"I guess I should find out," Flowers said. "What about you?"

Fargo shook his head.

"I've swung my last bat."

"Too bad about that," Flowers said, walking away, "you're a natural."

14

Despite the fact that the men from the East were ath-
letes, they were a bedraggled lot by the time they
pulled into Colorado Springs.

"Finally," one of them said, when the town came
into view, "civilization."

"If you can call it that," Catfish Hawkins said.

They had encountered no trouble on the trail, neither with Indians nor outlaws, and the wagons had
stood up to the trip so far. Supplies had become
somewhat depleted, but not as depleted as the men
were feeling.

"How long do we get to stay here?" Leo Gordon
called out to Fargo.

"I don't know that that's up to me," Fargo said.
"Mike will have something to say about it."

"We have to play here?" someone called out. "I
don't think I could lift a bat, let alone swing one."

"A day off will do wonders for all of you," Mike
Flowers called out, "and then we can play."

They pulled into town and stopped in front of the
livery. They attracted a lot of attention driving
down the main street, and Fargo thought he knew
now what circus people felt like when they arrived

in a Western town. Of course, there was no outward indication that the six wagons held baseball players. Apparently, getting that information out was Bridget's job.

"I'll see you all at the hotel," she said, as they pulled up in front of the livery.

"Where are you going?" Fargo asked.

"I have to get word out, talk to whatever newspapers are in town."

"You won't find as many as there were in Kansas City," Fargo said.

"That's fine."

"And you shouldn't be walking around alone," he added.

"Why, Fargo," she said, batting her eyes at him, "are you worried about me?"

"I'm just trying to head off trouble," Fargo said. "Willy?"

"Yes, sir?"

"Go with Miss Arnold."

"Yes, sir." Willy didn't have to be told twice. He'd apparently been smitten with Bridget ever since he first saw her.

"My hero," Bridget said playfully. "Come on, Willy. I'll hold on to your arm like you're my boyfriend."

"Aw, Miss Bridget—"

"Bri," Bridget said, as they walked away, "just call me Bri, Willy."

"All right, Miss Bridget . . ."

"That boy's got it bad," Flowers said with a grin.

"Mike," Fargo stated, "how are we going to get rooms for all these men?"

"Not your worry, Fargo," Flowers said.

"It's not?"

"No," Flowers said. "Your job ends when we get to a town, and picks up again when we leave one. You just have to get us where we're going in one piece. After that, I take over."

Fargo couldn't argue with that. It took him off the hook for the whole time they were in Colorado Springs, or any other town for that matter.

"Hope that doesn't bother you?" Flowers asked.

"Doesn't bother me at all, Mike."

"I didn't think it would," Flowers replied. "Why don't you just get yourself a room and we'll take care of everything else."

"I'll get a room after I take care of my horse," Fargo said, "and, if you don't mind, I'll stick around until I'm sure all of the horses are cared for, and the wagons are safe."

"Fine," Flowers said. "Let's get to it, then."

"I just thought of something," Fargo said, as he and Flowers left the livery half an hour later.

"What?"

"Money."

"Don't have to worry about that, either," Flowers said. "Bri's here to handle that."

"That's what I thought," Fargo said. "Is she walking around with money in her pockets?"

"She's got some," Flowers said, "but they're mostly bank drafts. She just needs to visit a bank each time we get to a town."

"And then she'll have money in her pockets."

"Right."

"Doesn't that worry you?"

"No," Flowers said. "She's got twenty-six body-guards, Fargo."

"None of whom are with her right now."

"Willy's with her."

"Willy's a kid, Mike," Fargo said. "If anything goes wrong—"

"Nothing'll go wrong, Fargo. Stop worrying," Flowers said. "Once she gets to the bank I'll have a couple of the boys stay with her all the time."

"All the time?"

"Well," Flowers said, "not *all* the time . . ."

"That's another thing," Fargo said. "She might be one of the boys out on the trail, but once we get to town she needs to have her own room."

"You and she can stay in a hotel," Flowers said. "My orders are to get the boys into rooming houses whenever I can. That's where Jack decided to scrimp and save."

"Okay," Fargo said, "I'll go to the hotel and get two rooms."

"Fine."

"You should get a room, too, Mike."

"That's okay, Fargo," the manager said. "I prefer to stay where the boys stay."

"Suit yourself."

"You go on ahead. I'll get the boys together."

"Try and stay out of trouble."

"Who's gonna start up with twenty-six men with baseball bats?" Flowers asked.

"Maybe nobody in Philadelphia, or Boston, but this is the West. There are men who would take that kind of thing as a challenge. Just keep your eyes open."

"Yes, sir," Flowers said, and saluted.

Fargo walked away, thinking that he liked Flowers pretty well after being together the better part of two weeks, but then he'd liked Ben Meeker almost right away, and look what had happened with that. He still felt bad about having apparently misjudged Meeker. He'd reserve his opinions about Flowers for a while.

Fargo went to one of the hotels in town and got two rooms. Now all he had to do was find Bridget Arnold and let her know which one she was in.

"The other room is for a woman," Fargo said. "I'll just put her name here and she'll be in later."

"Yes, sir. Do you want a key to her room as well?" The clerk was young and the question seemed innocent enough.

"No," Fargo said, after a moment, "just one key, for her."

"Yes, sir. I'll take care of the lady when she arrives."

"Thanks."

Fargo went to his room and left his saddlebags and rifle there. Then he turned around and went back out to find the nearest saloon.

Fargo found a saloon and settled down with a beer. He was standing at the bar with it when a man came running into the saloon.

"There's a baseball team in town!"

The place was less than half filled, and only a few men looked up from their drinks or their cards. Fargo looked at the man who had just entered and saw that he was about nineteen or so—Willy's age.

"What in hell is a baseball team?" one man asked.

"Don't you never read?" the boy asked. "It's a game from back East played with a ball and a bat—"

"What's a bat?" the man asked, and he and a few of his friends laughed.

"Mister?" the boy said to Fargo. "You know what I'm talkin' about, don't ya?"

"I sure do."

The boy took the news happily.

"You know what baseball is?" He wanted to be sure.

"Yes, I do, son," Fargo said, turning now to face the room. "It's a game that's sweeping the country. It's going to be real popular."

"See?" the boy glowed. "He knows what it is."

"So, what's this baseball team doin' here, then?" another man asked.

"They're passin' through, and they're gonna play a game tomorrow."

Tomorrow? Fargo thought. *Was Flowers going to have these men in shape to play tomorrow*?

"Where'd you hear about this, son?" Fargo asked.

"I was over at the newspaper office," he said. "I deliver papers for them. This real pretty lady came in and started tellin' Mr. Teasdale—he's the editor—all about it."

"And she said they were going to play tomorrow?" Fargo asked.

"She sure did."

"Hey, kid," one man yelled, "is this pretty lady gonna play?"

"I don't know if it's a game for girls," the boy said, "but she's gonna be there."

"How pretty is she?" someone else asked.

"She's real pretty!"

"Maybe this baseball game'll be somethin' to see," the first man said.

"I gotta go," the boy said excitedly. "Mr. Teasdale wants me to pass the news, and then it's gonna be in tomorrow mornin's paper."

Fargo finished his beer and left the saloon before someone asked him how he knew about baseball. He didn't want anybody thinking maybe he was a shill for the game and getting mad about it later. By tomorrow, he didn't think anyone would remember he was in the saloon.

15

Fargo started looking for Bridget Arnold. He decided to try the hotel first, just in case she'd found it on her own. She wasn't there, though.

By checking around, he found out that she had been at the offices of both town newspapers for publicity purposes. After visiting both places he went to the telegraph office, and that's where he found her.

"There you are," he said.

"Fargo," she replied, "I was just finishing up here. You been looking for me?"

"All over town."

She smiled, her face lighting up.

"Worried about me?" she asked coyly.

"Just wanted to let you know what hotel you're in," Fargo said. "Where's Willy? Maybe he's the one I should be worried about."

"He's with some of the boys. They got him a room at the same rooming house they're staying in."

"Here you go, miss," the clerk said, handing her what looked like a telegram.

"Thank you." She turned to Fargo, tucking the

telegram into her shirt pocket. "Had to check in with the boss."

"Your father?"

"He's the boss," she said. "Never lets me forget it, too. You want to tell me what hotel I'm in, or walk me over there?"

"I'll walk with you," he said, "keep you out of trouble."

"Sounds like a good idea."

When they got outside she linked her arm in his. Like he was her boyfriend.

"Why did you take this job?" she asked him.

"I've thought about that myself quite a bit before we left Kansas City," he said. "I decided it was a combination of curiosity, and boredom."

"Do you get bored easily?"

"Only if I'm in one place for too long a period of time."

"I get that way, too," she said. "That's why I prefer to travel with the team."

"You've been doing that for a long time?"

"Oh, yes."

"You get along with the fellas on the team?"

"With most of them," she replied. "They treat me like I'm their sister—well, the ones who aren't trying to get me into bed."

"How many is that?"

"How many are trying? Not as many as there used to be. No, lately only Catfish seems to think I should be going to bed with him."

"What would your father think of that?"

"Well," she answered, "he is the team's best pitcher."

"Does that mean he would want you to lie down with him in order to keep him happy?"

"No," she said, "my father knows that the decision about who I spend my time with has always been mine."

"Have you told Catfish you won't spend the night with him?"

"Why would I do that?" she asked. "Then he'd stop trying. A girl likes to be pursued, Fargo."

"I heard that," he said, "I just didn't know if it also was true of Eastern girls."

"Any woman wants to be pursued," she said, "but she'll pick very carefully the man she wants to actually be caught by."

"Women are the same everywhere, aren't they?"

As they mounted the boardwalk she released his arm and turned to face him.

"Why do I feel that you are more qualified to answer that question than I am?"

She went into the lobby ahead of him.

They stopped at her door, and she abruptly turned to face him, putting her hand on his chest.

"Come inside with me."

"That wouldn't be wise."

"Why not?"

"Because I work for your father."

"Are you afraid of him?"

"What do you think?"

"I know you're not . . . so come inside."

"What if some of the players find out," he said, "or Flowers? What if your father found out?"

She undid one button on his shirt and slipped her hand inside.

"My God, you're so firm."

Her hand was hot on his chest. Suddenly, her left hand moved down between his legs.

"*Very* firm," she said, softly, licking her lips seductively. Her lower lip was very ripe. He wondered if her peach-sized breasts were as perky as they looked.

"I told you," she said, moving both her hands in small circles, "who I sleep with is my business, not my father's."

At that moment they heard voices on the stairs. Willy was saying to someone, "I told you, Mike, it was them comin' in here."

Willy and Flowers. Bridget yanked her hand out of Fargo's shirt and from his crotch just as the two men reached the top of the stairs.

"Let's finish this conversation, later," she said huskily, and went into her room.

"What's on your mind, boys?" Fargo asked, turning to face Flowers and Willy.

"Want to eat dinner with Willy, me, and the boys?" Flowers asked.

"I don't think so," Fargo said. "The hotel's got a dining room. You're probably going to eat at the boarding house, and I'm not a guest there. I'll get something here."

"Maybe you can eat with Bri," Flowers said, "since she's staying here, too."

"Maybe I'll do that."

"See ya later," Willy called out as he and Flowers started down the hall.

Fargo made a show of going to his room, closing the door loudly behind him. He thought briefly about knocking on Bridget's door once Willy and

Flowers had left, but he decided against it. Sleeping with the boss's daughter was never a good idea. Of course, that didn't keep her from knocking on his door later.

When he heard the knock nearly half an hour later, he opened the door. She immediately rushed in, closed the door, and leaned back against it. She was still wearing her jeans and shirt, but she was breathing heavily.

"My guess is you weren't going to come to my room," she said, "so I came to yours."

"Bridget—"

She started unbuttoning her shirt and peeled it off. She was naked beneath it, and her little breasts were round and firm, tipped by hard, pink nipples.

"You want to kick me out? Huh?" she dared him.

He didn't answer. At that moment she was the most erotic thing he'd ever seen. She undid her jeans and skinned them down her legs, kicking them off. It was then he realized she'd come over barefoot. The smell of her filled the room, and engorged his senses.

"Want me to go?" she asked, sliding closer to him. Her hand went down to his crotch. "Oh, I see you don't want me to go."

"No," he said hoarsely.

She smiled, licked her lips, and dropped to her knees. She undid his pants and pulled them down, letting him spring free. With a sound somewhere between a growl and a groan she was on him, licking him, stroking him, rubbing her hard breasts up and down one thigh and then the other.

He reached for her, put his hands under her arms

and lifted her until her feet were off the floor, then turned and deposited her on the bed. In record time, he kicked off his boots and pants, stripped off his shirt, and crawled into the bed.

Her body was taut and sleek, firm everywhere, but smooth and sweet-smelling, like honeysuckle. He bit her nipples, sucked them into his mouth, then licked her breasts, rubbing against her cleft, enjoying the way her downy hair felt on him.

"Oooh, Fargo, yes," she moaned, "I knew this would happen, right from that first day . . . yesssss . . ."

She began moving her hips as they rubbed together, skin against skin, until, with a flick of both their hips, he was suddenly inside of her.

"Ohhh," she gasped, biting her lip. "Yes, yes, yes, do it, harder . . . come on, come on . . ." she implored him through clenched teeth, "come on . . . yes, yes, oh, yes . . ."

Over and over again he plunged into her as she lifted her hips to meet him, gasping and groaning and swearing until suddenly she was bucking beneath him, trapped in pleasure, then he was exploding inside her, filling her with what felt like millions of tiny hot needles and he felt as if his whole body were going to explode. . . .

They lay side by side on the bed for a while, catching their breath. He was lying on his stomach, she on her back, stroking his buttocks with one hand.

"In Kansas City, in front of the livery, I saw you and all I wanted to do was go into that barn with you and get naked."

He laughed and said, "That would never have worked, Bridget."

"It would have been fun," she said, "trying to do this quietly with all those men waiting outside for us."

"Yeah, real fun," he said. "You told me they were like your brothers. They probably would have torn me apart for doing what they all want to do."

"Well," she said, digging her nails into his rear and laughing, "it would have been fun for me . . ."

She wanted to make love again, but he jumped up off the bed and said, "I'm hungry. You've made me ravenous."

He reached for his pants.

"Actually," she said, "I'm hungry too." She reclined on her back, absently scratching her stomach. "But after we eat, we come right back here."

"That sounds like an order." Fargo smiled.

She sat up and said, "I can make it one. Remember, I represent my father here."

He looked at her and said, almost seriously, "Well, not in *here*!"

They went down to the hotel dining room and ordered a lot of food. They were both starving, tearing into their food as if they hadn't eaten in weeks when, in truth, Dutch had been feeding them quite well. The kind of frantic, desperate lovemaking they'd shared simply built up an appetite in each of them that was hard to satisfy.

Later, over pie and coffee Fargo said, "We can't let Dutch know we ate like this."

"I know," she said. "He's such a sweet man, it would break his heart."

From where he sat Fargo could see through the lobby to the street in front.

"It's still light out."

"I know," she said.

"Flowers, or Willy, or somebody else might still come looking for us."

They finished their dessert and looked across the table at each other, another kind of hunger coursing through them.

"We can just ignore it if someone knocks on the door," she said.

"If we even hear it," he said.

They went back up to his room.

16

The game was played the next day to an enthusiastic crowd. They didn't see how exhausted the players were from their journey. Even to Fargo's unpracticed eye, the players looked sloppy and weary.

But Bridget had done her job well, and the people turned out—and paid—to watch and cheer.

And so it went at the next three towns where they stopped and played until, weeks later, they came to Carson City, Nevada.

"The team can't play."

Fargo, Flowers, and Bridget looked up from their dinner together.

"What?" Flowers started.

Leo Gordon, the team spokesman, said, "We're too tired. All of us. Jenkins has a pulled muscle that hasn't been able to heal, Jones's hand is fractured, and the rest of us are plumb bushed."

"Take them both to the doctor," Bridget said.

"We can do that," Gordon said, "but a doctor is not going to heal them by tomorrow."

"We'll have to skip the game—" Flowers started, but Bridget interrupted him.

113

"No. We have to play!" she snapped.

"Skip." Gordon said, speaking directly to Flowers. "These injuries wouldn't be happening if we weren't playing tired. I know it."

"Traveling cross-country and playing may have been a bad idea," Flowers said.

"Tell that to my father," Bridget said. "If you've got the guts."

Along the way, Fargo had seen displays of temper from Bridget which he had put down to just that—temperament. Now, however, he was seeing more clearly that she was indeed her father's daughter.

"The men will play," she said, "or be kicked off the team."

Flowers shook his head and said, "You can't kick them *all* off—"

"We'll get a new team, if we have to," she said. "We'll send them by train to San Francisco if we must—along with a new manager."

She threw her napkin down and stood up.

"I'm sending a telegraph message to my father," she said with finality. "Let's see what he has to say about all this."

She stormed out of the hotel dining room, and Gordon sat down.

"If they fire us," he asked, "will they pay our way back home? Or will they leave us stranded here?"

"Nobody's getting fired, Leo," Flowers assured him. He looked at Fargo expectantly.

"What do you expect me to do?" Fargo asked him.

"You're sleeping with her."

Fargo gave him a surprised look.

"Oh, it's not like the whole team doesn't know it," Flowers said.

Fargo looked at Gordon this time.

"It's true," he said. "We always know when she's, well, being . . . satisfied."

Fargo didn't like the sound of that, but he let it go for the moment. "I still don't know what I can do."

"Talk to her," Flowers said. "Make her see how silly it would be to have to get a new team now, after we've come all this way."

"And what about playing tomorrow?"

Flowers said, "We can field a couple of teams without using the injured men." Now he looked at Gordon.

"It won't be very pretty," the catcher said.

"It hasn't been the whole way," Flowers said. "Let's just hope we can get enough rest when we get to San Francisco before we have to play another team."

"Another team?" Fargo asked. "What other team?"

"A local team," Flowers said. "That's why Jack wanted us to go overland, so he could use the time to drum up a local team in San Francisco to play us."

"And then?"

Flowers shrugged.

"We'll play. The locals will root for their team."

Suddenly, it hit Fargo. "And they bet on them, too, won't they?"

Flowers shrugged.

"Possibly."

"Doesn't that bother you?"

"Why should it?" he asked. "Jack has bet on us before."

"But has he bet *against* you before?"

"What are you talking about?"

"You said it yourself. Your team is tired, and they'll be even more tired when they get to San Francisco."

Flowers looked at Gordon.

"Leo, why don't you go and see about getting those men to a doctor."

"What should I tell the team?"

"Nothing," Flowers said, "I'll be along in a while to talk to them myself."

"Okay, Skipper," the catcher said, and left.

"Do you think that's what Jack is doing?" Flowers asked Fargo, urgently. "Setting us up to lose so he can make a killing?"

"Sounds like it to me," Fargo said.

"That son of a bitch! And then maybe he will leave us stranded in San Francisco."

"He's got the money," Fargo said. "He can always buy another team."

"That son of a bitch!" Flowers yelled again.

"His daughter is a little like him, isn't she?" Fargo asked.

"Finding that out, are you?" Flowers asked. "Yeah, little Bridget's been on her best behavior with you . . . up until now."

"I guess I'd better talk to her, then," Fargo said.

"Just slow her down, some," Flowers said, "Put her at ease . . . maybe tire her out some. I'll bet you know how you can do that."

Fargo gave him a short look that said, *Back off*, and Flowers did.

"Just do your best, that's all I'm saying," Flowers said quietly.

"What will you do about tomorrow?"

"We'll play," Flowers replied. "Willy's been working out with us. Maybe I'll let him play."

"That'll give him a thrill," Fargo said.

"I know it."

"I'll see you later."

Fargo left the Carson House, where he and Bridget were staying, and went looking for her. They had continued taking separate rooms since Colorado Springs, but for the most part they used one every night. Fargo had suspected that a few members of the team might have to know about it, but now he knew that everyone did.

And they didn't care.

So much for her being everybody's sister.

Fargo caught Bridget coming out of the telegraph office.

"I didn't get an answer back right away," she said. "We'll have to wait."

"For what?"

"To see what my father wants to do."

"Why don't you just decide?" he asked. "You're his representative, aren't you?"

"Like I said, he's the boss."

"But while you're here," Fargo said, "you're the boss. Why don't you just make a decision?"

"These lazy idiots want to take a day off," she said. "We can't afford that."

"These lazy idiots are like your brothers," he reminded her, "or so you say."

"I never said that," she replied, folding her arms over her breasts.

"Yes, you did."

"No, I didn't," she said, firmly. "I know exactly what I said."

"What did you say, then?"

"I said *they treat me* like a sister."

"Isn't that the same thing?"

"No," she said, "because I don't treat them like my brothers. To me, they're employees of my father's."

"And that's how you treat them?"

"Yes," she said, "and if they don't play tomorrow, they get fired."

"That's the decision your father would make?"

"Yes."

"Wouldn't you like to make a decision on your own?" he asked.

"Why?" she asked.

"To show everybody that you can."

"Are you under the impression that I'm trying to prove something to somebody?"

"Aren't you?"

She laughed and said, "No. I know exactly what I'm doing with my life, Fargo. It's what I want to do with it."

"Work for your father forever?"

"For as long as I want," she said. "He knows that, and he accepts it."

"Do you have any brothers or sisters?"

"No," she said, "and I don't want any. If you want to know if I have a mother, the answer is no, she died, and I don't want one."

"Do you want a father?"

"I don't have a choice," she said. "I have one, and that's that. Did they send you to talk to me? Do you think that you'll have some influence over me because we're sharing the same bed?"

"Maybe they did," Fargo said, "but I didn't."

She moved closer to him and put her hand on his arm.

"Speaking of which, why don't we just go and do that right now and forget about all this?"

"You've got a couple of injured employees, Bridget. They may injure themselves even more tomorrow if you make them play. What would your father say about that?"

She appeared to think about that for a while.

"Well," she finally said, "I don't want them being so hurt they can't ever play."

"You're going to need all of your men when you get to San Francisco."

"You have a point, Fargo," she said. "All right, I'll talk to Flowers. The injured men don't have to play, but there has to be a game."

"If that's your decision."

"It is. See, I'm not so hard to get along with, am I?" she asked.

"Not so long as you don't treat me like an employee," he said.

"Oh," she said, "you're more than that, Fargo, *much* more that that. Later, I'll show you how much."

"Why not show me now?" he asked. "I thought you wanted to—"

"I forgot." She cut him off. "I have to go to the bank and draw out the bulk of the money we'll need for San Francisco."

"Why not wait until we get there?"

"I just . . . want to get it out now," she said. "I'll see you at the hotel."

═════════ 17 ═════════

Fargo found Flowers at the hotel and discovered that he'd already talked with Bridget.

"I don't know what you said, but it worked. The two players who are hurt can sit, and I'll use Willy."

"Good," Fargo said, "he'll enjoy that."

"Bri was on her way to the bank," Flowers said. "Wonder why she's taking the money out now?"

"I asked, too," Fargo said. "She didn't have an answer."

"Guess she can do what she wants. I'm heading to the saloon. Want a drink?"

"Sure."

They walked out of the hotel together, and then suddenly, Fargo grabbed Flowers by the arm.

"What is it?" the manager asked.

"Those two men across the street."

"What about them?"

"Those are the Benedict brothers," Fargo said. "The two men who were angry that I didn't hire them back in Kansas City."

"What are they doing here?"

"I don't know," Fargo said, "but I'm going to find out. It can't just be a coincidence."

"What are you going to do?" Flowers asked.

"Follow them."

"Want me to come along?"

"Do you have a gun?"

"No."

"Then go on to the saloon and I'll meet you there."

"Is there going to be trouble?"

"I hope not, Mike," Fargo said. "Go on. I don't want to lose them."

Fargo stepped down from the boardwalk and hurried after the Benedict boys, leaving a worried Mike Flowers behind.

Fargo just couldn't accept that these two could be in Carson City by any accident or coincidence. They had to be here by design, but why? For what reason?

As he followed them, though, it soon became clear. They led him right to the bank, and as they got there, Bridget was coming out the front door.

Now he was dead sure this was no coincidence, but how had they known that the team would be here, and that Bridget would be going to the bank?

They stopped across the street and Fargo stepped into a doorway down the street from them so he wouldn't be seen. Fargo noticed that one of them was sporting a bandage on his head.

The two men gave Bridget a head start, then crossed the street and started afer her. Fargo followed. He didn't want to get too close, but he also couldn't hang back too far, just in case they tried something. He didn't want Bridget getting hurt because he didn't have enough time to reach her.

They went three blocks this way and then Bridget

stopped and seemed to be counting the money she'd taken out of the bank—right on the street!

Suddenly, the two men quickly closed the distance between them and her, took hold of her, and pulled her into an alley that was right there.

Fargo cursed and broke into a run. He reached the alley and turned into it, drawing his gun. He expected to hear Bridget yelling, but didn't. Maybe they had a hand over her mouth . . . but then he heard their voices.

He crept deeper into the alley and was able to make out the words.

". . . get it all?" one man said.

"Yes, I got it all," Bridget replied. "Don't grab it from me!"

"Just give it here!" the man shouted.

Fargo moved in closer. The alley was a dead end, stopping in front of a fence, and there stood Bridget surrounded by three men—the Benedict boys . . . and Ben Meeker.

"Hold it!" Fargo shouted.

The three men turned their head and saw him. The Benedict boys each went for their guns. Fargo had no choice but to shoot.

His first shot hit Dirk—or was it Dack?—in the chest. He coughed, stumbled, and fell. Then Fargo turned his gun on Dack—or was it Dirk?—who was still trying to claw his gun from his holster.

"Stop!" Fargo shouted, but the young man wouldn't heed the warning, so Fargo fired. The bullet struck the man in the belly. He dropped his gun and fell to the ground. His hat fell off, revealing his bandaged head.

Ben Meeker was wearing a gun, but he hadn't

drawn it. He backed up until his back was against the fence, gripping the money tightly in his hands.

"Don't!" he shouted. "Wait! It's not what you—"

Fargo held his fire, but Bridget had picked up one of the fallen brother's guns and she pulled the trigger, hitting Meeker in the shoulder.

"Bridget!" Fargo shouted.

"No!" Meeker protested, but she shot him again, and this time the bullet went through his right eye, killing him instantly.

Bridget dropped the gun and ran to the fallen man. She got on her knees and started picking up the money that had fallen from his lifeless hands.

"You son of a bitch!" she hissed at his dead form. "Give me my money!"

Fargo checked the two brothers to make sure they too were dead, then walked over to Meeker's body. He holstered his gun and helped Bridget up.

"Are you all right?" he asked.

"Yes," she said, putting her head against his chest. "They grabbed me and pulled me in here. I thought they were . . . were going to kill me."

"I think they just wanted the money," he said, "although I don't know how they knew we'd be here."

"Who were they?"

"Those two were the Benedict brothers," Fargo said, "and the man you killed was Ben Meeker. They're all from Kansas City."

"Did they follow us?" she asked.

"If they did," he said, "I don't know why they waited this long to try and rob you. You went to the bank in each town."

"Yes, but here I got the most money out," she

pointed out, then added, "but how would they know I was going to do that?"

"I don't know," Fargo said. "Come on, let's go and find the sheriff and tell him what happened here. Are you sure you're all right?"

"I'm fine, thanks to you," she said gratefully, and they left the alley and went looking for the local law.

The match went off as planned, with Willy playing a surprisingly good game at second base. The players were dragging, though, but nobody seemed to realize or mind. None of the players had been told of the attempted robbery, only Flowers.

Afterward Flowers came up to Fargo while the players were gathering up the equipment.

"If we had to play anybody else other than ourselves today," he said, "we would have gotten beat, bad."

"Nobody here seemed to notice anything."

"You can be sure Bridget noticed," he said. "She notices everything."

"Why did I have the impression that," Fargo asked, "for most of this trip, everybody liked her?"

"That's the impression they wanted you to have," Flowers said. "Nobody will tell you the truth about her because they don't want to get fired."

"You're telling the truth, though."

"She got me good and mad yesterday," Flowers said, "insisting that even the injured players had to play. Whatever you said or did—"

"Sacrifices," Fargo said, "I had to make many sacrifices."

Flowers laughed and said, "Oh yeah, I'll just bet you did. Still, I can't help feeling sorry for her. She didn't deserve to be robbed like that, maybe even killed. It's a good thing you recognized those two men."

"Yeah," Fargo said, "a good thing."

"How'd they get here?" Flowers said. "And what about that other man, Meeker? What was his part?"

"My guess is they were working for Meeker, and he was the one who decided to rob Bridget as she left the bank."

"Yeah, but why this bank? In this town?"

"That I don't know," Fargo said. "All three men are dead. I wanted to take Meeker alive. He didn't draw his gun, but Bridget killed him."

"I guess she was just too scared to notice," Flowers said.

"Yeah," Fargo said, "she was scared, I guess."

"Did she send a telegram to her father to let him know what happened?"

"I don't think so," Fargo said. "I don't think she wants him to know."

"Well, maybe that's best for now," Flowers said. "I'm going to see to my boys, Fargo."

"I'll see you later."

Fargo couldn't help wishing he'd been able to take Meeker alive. The way things stood now, they'd probably never know the whole story—and it would eat at him for a long time.

There was that damned curiosity of his, again.

18

When they pulled out of town the next morning Bridget was very quiet, and avoided Fargo's eyes. He wondered if she was feeling bad over killing a man, or if there was entirely something else on her mind.

He was riding next to the wagon that Flowers was driving.

"How are your boys tody?"

"Tired, but excited to be on the last leg of the trip to San Francisco."

"That's good."

"They're also curious."

"About what?"

"Well, they've heard all these stories about the Wild West, and yet we haven't run into a lick of trouble."

"And they want to?"

"Well, no . . . not exactly," Flowers said. "I guess they're just curious . . . you know . . ."

"Well, tell them we still have a ways to go," Fargo said. "There's still time for something to happen."

Fargo wasn't sure, but Flowers himself seemed to brighten at the prospect. What Fargo didn't know at the moment was just how prophetic his words would be.

"Hold up!" Fargo raised his hand and stopped the forward motion of the small wagon train. Then he rode a bit ahead of them and stopped. He was so intent on what he was looking at that Flowers coming up next to him actually startled him.

"What is it?" the manager asked. "What's wrong?"

Fargo looked down at him, then off into the distance again.

"I can't be sure," he said. "Maybe that trouble you were looking for."

"What do you see?"

"Some smoke," Fargo said, "and dust."

"Smoke and dust? What does that mean?" Flowers shaded his eyes with his hand and peered into the distance. "I don't see it."

"I do," Fargo said. "Stay here, and keep everyone in the wagons."

"Where are you going?"

"To take a look."

As Fargo started away Flowers shouted, "Wait! What do we do if you don't come back?"

"Keep heading west," Fargo called back.

As Fargo drew nearer, the smoke became more evident. It had been a wisp when it caught his attention, but there had been enough there to make him cautious.

He reined in the Ovaro just short of topping a rise and dismounted. He'd go the rest of the way on foot. When he got to the top of the rise he went down on his belly and observed what was going on.

There was carnage below him. Several wagons had been burned, and there were bodies strewn about. Moving among the bodies were a band of Comancheros, taking everything that wasn't nailed down. Comancheros were an odd breed of men who were not claimed by the Indians or the whites. They existed as scavengers, and didn't care who they scavenged from.

From his vantage point Fargo could see that there were children among the dead, and the women were naked. The three wagons had been filled with families. The Comancheros had killed the men and children, then raped and killed the women—maybe not in that order. Maybe they made the men and children *watch* the rape and murder of their wives and mothers.

Obviously, these families had crossed paths with the Comancheros and had not lived to regret it.

He took a head count, then crept back down to his horse, mounting up. He proceeded first at walk so as not to be heard and then, when he was far enough away, at a gallop.

When he got back he could see that his orders had not been obeyed. Half the players were milling about outside the wagons, Bridget and Flowers among them.

"What are you doing out of your wagons?"

"It's hot in there," Bridget said. "If we're just going to sit here I for one am not going to roast inside these wagons."

"What did you find?" Flowers asked.

"Comancheros," he said. "A dozen of them."

"What's a Comanchero?" one of the players asked.

"Something you don't want to run into," Fargo said, "and there are a dozen of them."

"Well, there's more of us than them," another player said.

"That's true," Fargo said, "but they can shoot."

"What makes you think they'll want trouble?" Bridget asked.

"Because," Fargo said, "they just killed three families, and then burnt their wagons."

"That was the smoke you saw?" Flowers asked.

"That was it."

"How do we avoid them?" the manager asked.

"We may not have to," Fargo said. "If we get lucky they'll go a different way."

"And if they don't?" Bridget asked.

"Then we've got big trouble," Fargo said, "because not enough of you can shoot to make a difference."

"So what do we do?" Flowers asked.

"I gave that some thought on the way back," Fargo said. "Here's what I want to do . . ."

"Bascially," Flowers said, after his explanation, "this is what you call a bluff."

"I know."

"Can you bluff Comancheros?" he asked.

"That I don't know," Fargo admitted, "but we're going to find out. Everyone get into your wagons. Mike?"

"Yeah?"

"I want you, Catfish, and Gordon in the front wagon, and Bridget and Willy in the next one."

"Why?"

"Because you five can shoot. I want to spread you out."

"A few of the others can shoot, as well."

"I know," Fargo said. "Spread them out, too."

"All right."

Fargo walked ahead of the wagons, taking the Ovaro with him, and started off the way he had come. Bridget came up next to him.

"Tuck your hair up under your hat," he said.

"Why?"

"Because you don't want these men to know you're a woman."

He felt her shiver next to him. He looked at her. They had to do something about her body. It still obviously looked like it belonged to a woman.

"Let's go see Basher," he said, taking her arm.

"Why?"

"Because he's the biggest man on the team."

"And why do we want the biggest man on the team?"

"Because you'll want to borrow some of his clothes."

Once they had Bridget's womanly curves buried in one of Basher's shirts and a pair of his pants, and her hair buried beneath her hat, they were ready to go.

"With a little luck," Fargo said, again, "they'll head anywhere but east."

But, of course, he knew that they wouldn't. Everything had gone just a little too smoothly for that. If they got out of this alive he was going to tell Mike Flowers what a jinx he was.

"Here they come," Fargo said to Flowers, "heading right for us."

"Jesus," Flowers said, wiping his mouth on his sleeve.

"Take it easy, Mike," Fargo said. "If we go according to plan we can get out of this."

"Right, right."

"I'll tell the others. You tell everyone in your wagon."

"Right."

Fargo rode back to the other wagons and told them the Comancheros were heading straight for them.

"Just do what we planned," he called out.

He could see from the looks on their faces that they were nervous and scared. Maybe this would cure them of looking for some Wild West action.

He rode back to the front of the column.

"When do we stop?" Flowers asked. "We're getting real close."

"We'll let them stop first," Fargo said.

"What if they don't?"

"They will."

"Why?"

"Because they don't know what we have in our wagons. First, they'll want to find out if we've got anything worth fighting for."

"How can you be so sure?"

"It's what I'd do."

* * *

Finally, right about the time he could almost make out the features on some of them, the Comancheros stopped. Their leader held up a hand, bringing them to a halt.

"Okay, stop," Fargo called out.

Flowers reined in, and the others did the same behind them.

"Now what?"

"Now two or three of them will ride closer to talk," Fargo said.

Sure enough the leader and two others peeled off from the bulk of the goup and started riding forward.

"All right," Fargo called out, "bring the wagons around like we talked about."

The drivers all got their wagons going and by the time the Comancheros had reached them, the wagons were abreast, the horses facing south so that one side was facing the Comancheros.

Fargo could see that the leader was Mexican. One of the other men was white, and the second was an Indian, probably a renegade from some tribe Fargo couldn't identify at the moment.

They stopped.

"Señor?"

"What do you want?"

"You have many wagons, señor," the leader said. "Surely you can spare one or two."

"Why would I want to do that?" Fargo asked.

The man smiled wickedly, revealing many gold teeth, and some stained yellow ones as well.

"Because if you do not give up two of your wagons, señor," the man said, "we will take them all."

"How do you know there's anything in the wagons you'd want?"

"Why don't you tell us what's in the wagons, señor?" the man asked pointedly.

"Sure," Fargo said. "Guns."

"Ah!" The man's eyes widened. "Many guns?"

"Yes."

"What type?"

"Rifles."

"What kind?" the man asked.

"The kind that kill."

The man started laughing.

"You are very funny, señor. So, you have guns, we can use guns. We have a bargain, eh?"

"There's just one thing."

"What's that?"

Fargo raised his arms and suddenly the sides of the Conestogas were rolled up, and the men in the buckboards stood up. They were all holding guns. To someone who didn't know that most of these men couldn't hit the ground of the tribe, the baseball team looked formidable.

"I also have many men to use the guns."

The man's smile faded.

"We are not amused, señor."

"Neither are we," Fargo said. "Take your men and clear a path for us. We're coming through."

"No," the man said. "Why should we believe that these rifles can even shoot?"

Fargo raised his other hand. Someone fired. It was either Catfish, or Bridget, because they were the best shots.

The Comanchero leader was wearing a big sombrero with a high crown. Fargo saw the crown twitch as a bullet went through it. Maybe it even parted the man's hair.

"Aye," the leader said, "that is good shooting."

"Yes, it is."

He felt his sombrero, poking his finger through the hole.

"My men can shoot, also."

"We outnumber you two to one."

The leader paused, then nodded and said, "You do have more men then we, señor."

"What do you want to do?" Fargo said. "Move or die?"

"I still do not know that all these guns can fire," he said.

"If I show you they can what will you do?"

"If they all can fire," the leader said, "we would be foolish to challenge you. We would go and find easier prey."

Beyond the first three, the other Comancheros were growing restless. Fargo hoped the leader was speaking the truth. He didn't know how many men he had who would actually be willing to fire at another human being, even to save their own lives.

"I'll have them fire," Fargo said, "but I don't know where the shots will go."

"Señor, wait—"

Fargo waved his hand and suddenly the air erupted with gunfire. Each of the baseball team fired one shot, and it sounded like a barrage, as they didn't quite all fire at the same time. Fargo was concerned because he didn't even see a puff of dust, which meant no one had hit a thing. He hoped that meant they had fired in the air.

The Comanchero leader and his two compadres

had all flinched at the gunfire, and drawn their handguns. Fargo had his hand on his own gun. The next five seconds would be telling. He had it in his mind that he would fire at the leader first.

"You have a formidable force, señor," the leader finally said.

Those were his last words. He holstered his weapon, spoke to his *compadres,* and they all turned their horses and rode back to the main body of men.

"We did it," Flowers said.

"Not yet," Fargo said. "Just sit tight and let's see what they do."

The leader turned his horse, waved at Fargo as if to say good-bye—a grand gesture—and then all of the Comancheros turned their horses and rode south.

He hoped they wouldn't stop until they reached Mexico.

The air erupted again, this time with cheers. Fargo let them have their moment to scream and yell and expend all of the energy that their fear had built up, and then he turned and waved them quiet.

"Let's get these wagons pointed west again and head for San Francisco before they change their minds."

Everyone seemed to agree with that and the wagons started moving.

"Who fired?" Fargo asked Flowers.

"It was Catfish."

Fargo took a deep breath and said, "I take back every bad thing I ever said about him."

"I never heard you say anything."

"Well," Fargo said, "I was thinking it."

19

By the time they pulled into San Francisco, half the team was swearing off baseball. The claimed they were never going to play again, but they didn't say it within earshot of Bridget.

They drove the wagons to a prearranged livery stable and then Bridget gathered them just outside the building.

"I've got a surprise for you boys," she announced.

"What kind of surprise?" Flowers asked.

"You won't have to go looking for a rooming house," she said.

"Oh hell," Basher called out, "we got to sleep in the barn, boys."

Everyone laughed and Bridget said, "Not a barn, a first-class hotel!"

"What?" Flowers asked, and the others all looked around, puzzled.

"I convinced my father that you all deserved first-class accommodations after the journey you just made, because you never missed one game."

Suddenly, they were all cheering, even the men who'd just sworn they were going to quit.

"What hotel?" some asked.

"The Alhambra," she said, "right in the middle of Portsmouth Square."

Flowers moved up next to Fargo and asked pointedly, "Did you have anything to do with this?"

"Didn't know a thing about it," Fargo said honestly.

"It couldn't be her idea."

"How about Arnold?"

"It could be his," Flowers said, "but he'd have to be up to something."

"Well, maybe we'll find out what," Fargo said. "I wonder if this includes me."

"Well, you have to get paid off, so I'd say yes," Flowers said.

"I'll see you there, then."

The men were dispersing, already heading over to the Alhambra, and Flowers went to catch up. Willy came running up to Fargo.

"Fargo, Miss Bridget says this includes you and me!" he said excitedly. "I'm gonna have my own room in a big San Francisco hotel!"

"Try and stay out of trouble, will you, Willy?"

"Oh, Fargo . . . come on, ain't you gonna go over there?"

Fargo looked around and saw that Bridget was gone.

"I suppose so, Willy," he said, assuming he'd see her sometime that evening. "Let's go."

They left the livery, found a cab, and took it to the Alhambra, one of the biggest of the Portsmouth Square hotels and gambling houses.

When they got to the hotel, they discovered that there was, indeed, a room reserved for each of them.

Willy was so impressed by the huge lobby he just kept looking around, saying, "Wow!"

"If you keep that up," Fargo said, "people are going to think you've never been to a big city before."

"But I haven't," Willy said.

"Well, you don't want people to know that, do you?" Fargo asked.

"Why not?"

"Because they'll take advantage of you, Willy," Fargo said. "Just take my word for it and stop gaping at everything."

"Okay."

They got their keys and went upstairs to the second floor.

"I'm in room sixteen," Willy said. "Gee, that's all the way at the other end of the hall from you."

"You won't get lost," Fargo told him. "Go and take a look at your room and freshen up. Maybe even take a bath."

"A whole bath!"

"Well, just clean up, then, and meet me in the lobby and we'll get something to eat. We might as well stick together until we get paid by Jack Arnold."

"Okay."

"Meet me in half an hour."

Fargo watched Willy walk to his room, staring at the door for a few moments—probably a pop-eyed look of wonder on his face—before going in. He shook his head, turned, and walked to his own room.

* * *

In half an hour he was in the lobby, freshly bathed, wearing clean clothes, waiting for Willy. When the younger man appeared, he looked almost comical, his hair slicked down and combed with a part in the middle. His clothes were clean, but there was no denying they were trail clothes. He kept his eyes straight ahead as he walked toward Fargo.

"How do I look?" Willy asked. "Think anybody will know I never been to the big city now?"

"No one would ever have a clue, Willy. Come on, let's go into the dining room."

Willy let one "Wow" slip out as they entered the dining room, then got control of himself. They were shown to a table and gave their waiter their orders.

"Think it was all right to order steak?" Willy asked. "I never ate in the big city before."

"They'll have great steak here, Willy."

And they did. Willy raved about the meat and the vegetables—"Two kinds!"—as well as the biscuits, and marveled at how they served beer with dinners. After dinner, they had coffee and pie. Willy asked for rhubarb, saying he could never get rhubarb in a restaurant in Kansas City, and how his mother used to make it.

"He's just a little excited," Fargo told the waiter. "Bring him rhubarb, bring me peach."

"Yes, sir."

"You think he could tell—" Willy started to ask.

"Not a clue, kid," Fargo said.

At that moment, Bridget Arnold walked into the dining room and Fargo stared.

"I thought you told me not to stare at things like that—" Willy said, turning around, and seeing Bridget, he just stared.

Bridget had changed into a dress, and put her hair up. As she walked to the table, all eyes in the room followed her.

"I guess I'm too late for dinner," she said.

"You disappeared so quick this afternoon I didn't know what your plans were," Fargo said. "You look . . . wonderful."

"You look really pretty, Miss Bridget," Willy mumbled, completely in awe of her transformation.

"Can I sit?" she asked.

"Please do," Fargo offered.

"We were just gonna have dessert," Willy said. "Mine's rhubarb pie."

"That's nice, Willy. I came to give you both these." She took two envelopes out of the purse she was carrying and passed them over. "Payment in full."

Fargo accepted the envelope and said, "Thanks."

Willy opened his and again said, "Wow!"

"Don't take it out here, Willy," Fargo said. "Leave it in the envelope."

"This is more money than I ever seen!" Willy gasped.

"Just stay out of the casino with it," Bridget told him.

"If I gambled this money away," he said, "my mom would kill me. I'm gonna take it home and give it right to her."

"That's good, Willy," Bridget said, "real good." She looked at Fargo and asked, "Can we talk?"

"Sure," Fargo answered, "go ahead."

"No," she said. "I meant, alone."

"I got pie comin'," Willy said, mournfully. "You want me to leave?"

"Would you, Willy?" Bridget asked. "You're a

dear." She leaned over and kissed his cheek, and he immediately turned bright red and smiled dumbly.

"I'll bring your pie to your room, Willy," Fargo promised.

"That's okay, Fargo," the young man said, standing up. "Well, only if you remember," he then added.

"I will."

Willy waved at Bridget and said, "Bye, Miss Bridget."

"Bye, Willy."

He tripped on two chairs on his way out, but finally made it to the door without falling.

"What did you want to talk about?" Fargo asked her.

"My father would like you to come to his hotel tonight and talk to him."

"Really?" Fargo picked up the envelope and looked inside. The agreed-upon amount was inside. He put the envelope down.

"Why don't you tell your father that if he wants to talk to me, he'll have to come here," he said.

She looked startled for a moment, then said, "Well, all right, but my point was not *where* you spoke to him."

"It was what about."

"Right."

"You don't want me to tell him about the attempted robbery."

"Right."

"Or that you killed a man."

"God, no."

"Or," Fargo went on, "that you tried to rob him."

Bridget froze for a moment, then said, "I don't know what you—"

"Yes, you do, Bridget," Fargo said. "Come on, now. It took me a while to figure it out, but it shouldn't have taken that long."

"What are you talking about?" she asked. "Are you saying you think I wanted to rob my own father?"

"How much money did you get out of the bank in Carson City?"

"Twenty-five thousand."

"And the money you were taking out as we traveled from bank to bank. I'll bet you didn't use all that, did you."

"No, but—"

"So I'll bet you would have ended up with about forty thousand or so."

She didn't reply.

"Then you would have had to pay the Benedicts, and split the rest with Ben Meeker—or did Ben plan on killing them instead of paying them?"

"I think I should—"

He grabbed her by the wrist to keep her from leaving.

"If you don't want me to talk to your father, Bridget," he said, "you'll have to talk to me."

She settled back into her seat.

"All right."

"Was it Meeker's idea or yours?"

"Meeker? That dolt? It was mine. He took one look at me, and what I had to offer, and he went for the idea right away."

Fargo could believe that.

"He brought in those other two. My father's been

making me work for him for years and has been paying me next to nothing. I saw this as a chance to get some money out of him."

"Why stage a robbery? Why not just keep it like you were keeping money all along?"

"It was too much," she said. "My father would have questioned it."

"So somewhwere along the line, when you realized where our last stop would be before we crossed into California, you telegraphed Meeker."

"He and those two idiots took the train and got there ahead of us."

"So when I came into the alley, you weren't arguing with them—"

"I was, actually," Bridget said. "Meeker was trying to grab the money away from me. There was no guarantee at that point that they weren't planning to kill me and keep the money."

"I doubt that Meeker would have traded you for the Benedict boys," Fargo said. "You were part of the deal, weren't you?"

She smirked and said, "He thought so."

"So now you have to give all that money to your father?"

She made a face and said, "Yes."

"And if he finds out—"

"He'll disown me. I'll have less than the nothing I have now. At least now I'd get everything if he died."

"And what will you do for money in the meantime?"

"I'll wait for another chance—unless you tell him what happened."

"Would he believe me?"

She snorted and replied, "In a minute. He doesn't trust anyone."

Fargo sat back and thought it over for a few moments. The only person she would have hurt by taking that money would have been Jack Arnold. Of course, Meeker probably would have killed both the Benedict boys. He remembered that Meeker was trying to say something just before she shot him. He said, "It's not what you—" probably trying to tell Fargo it wasn't what he thought it was.

And then she'd killed him in cold blood.

"Well?" she asked. "Are you going to tell him?"

He stood up from the table and said, "You know what? I'm not sure," and walked away.

20

That night, Jack Arnold came to the Alhambra to see Fargo. Arnold found him in the casino, playing some blackjack.

"You came," Fargo said.

"Don't think you made me come, Fargo," Arnold said. "I was coming here to gamble, anyway."

It was a lie, and they both knew it.

"Would you step to the bar and have a drink with me? I want to talk to you."

"Sure," Fargo said, "why not?" He picked up the chips he'd won so far.

"Gambling with the money I paid you, I see," Jack Arnold said, as they walked to the bar.

"That's what it's for."

"And doing well?"

"Very well."

When they got to the bar, Arnold ordered a brandy for himself and a beer for Fargo.

"What did you want to talk to me about?" Fargo asked.

"You did a good job getting the team here," Arnold said.

"Thanks."

"I've got a game lined up for them with some locals."

"I thought you might."

"What's that mean?"

"You made me drag those boys cross-country so that when they got here, you could match them against some local team, and bet against them."

Arnold looked startled.

"Why would I bet on a baseball game?"

"This is a betting town."

"And why would I bet against my own team?"

"Because they're supposed to be the professionals," Fargo said. "You'd get a better price."

Arnold didn't speak, but Fargo could see the little wheels turning in the man's head. Could he bet against his team now that Fargo knew about it?

"When are they scheduled to play?" Fargo asked.

"Tomorrow."

"Hardly time for them to recover," Fargo said. "I'd suggest you postpone the game for, say, three days from now. That should give them time."

"And why would I do that?"

"Because you don't want me passing the word about what you were planning to do."

"Why should I care?"

"Because, like I said, this is a gambling town. If the gamblers around here found out you were trying to cheat them, I wouldn't give much for your chances of getting out of town without at the very least a couple of broken legs."

Arnold frowned, thought a moment, then said, "Yes, I see your point."

"I thought you would."

"Ah well," Arnold said, "there's still money to be

made. The fact that you figured out my little scheme just makes me more determined, though, to ask you to work for me."

"Oh, no."

"Why? You haven't heard my offer."

"I don't care what your offer is, Jack," Fargo said. "Now that I know you, I don't like you. And I sure wouldn't want to work for you."

"I can offer you—"

Fargo raised a finger to stop the man and said, "We're not all governed by money, Jack. Save the offer for someone who cares."

Arnold finished his brandy and put the empty glass down.

"You're a remarkable man, Fargo."

"Flattery will get you nowhere."

"Well," Arnold said, "I must take my leave. I have an engagement with a lady."

"Enjoy it."

"I will," Arnold said. "You know her, as a matter of fact—or of her. It's the lady who was singing in Kansas City when we were there. Brenda Benet."

"Oh, yes . . ."

"She's opening tonight at the Empire. I'm going to listen, and then take her to my room for a repeat of what we had in Kansas City."

Fargo was grateful to Arnold for telling him that Brenda was in town. He'd go over to the Empire later to meet up with her, as they had planned. He knew whose room she would really be in tonight.

"I think you'll probably get what you had in Kansas City, Jack."

Up until that point, Fargo had intended to tell Jack Arnold that his daughter had tried to rob him.

His lie—his continued lie—about Brenda, however, sealed the man's fate. Somewhere down the line, Bridget Arnold was going to steal from her father, and Fargo wished her luck.

"Good night, Fargo."

"Good-bye, Jack."

Fargo watched as Jack Arnold started walking toward the casino exit, and he saw Bridget standing there waiting for him, looking lovely in a low-cut blue gown. He hurriedly left the bar and walked after Arnold.

He didn't stop the man, though, he simply followed him up the stairs, staying just behind him.

"Come along, Bridget," Arnold said as he swept past his daughter.

Bridget held back just long enough for Fargo to reach her.

"Did you—" she started.

"I didn't tell him a thing," he said to her. "Good luck."

"Thanks."

He didn't bother telling her that he hadn't done it for her.

LOOKING FORWARD!
The following is the opening
section from the next novel in the exciting
Trailsman series from Signet:

**THE TRAILSMAN #211
BADLANDS BLOODBATH**

> *1861, the Badlands,
> a fitting name if ever there was one . . .*

Death had a name.

Between the Kansas Territory to the north and
Texas to the south lay a wasteland of living death
known as the Badlands. It was bad country, plain
and simple. There was little water, little vegetation.
The soil was too poor to support crops. Stark hills
and random buttes were crisscrossed by steep gul-
lies and deep ravines, creating a maze for the unwary traveler. No one in his right mind ever went
into the Badlands.

So Skye Fargo was all the more surprised when
he crossed the trail of a heavily laden wagon that
appeared to be doing just that. Puzzled, the big man
in buckskins reined up and dismounted. His pierc-
ing lake blue eyes raked the ground.

Hoofprints left in the wagon's wake told him a
cow plodded along behind it, probably tied to the
gate. The tracks were similar to those of a buffalo,
only smaller, the cloven hoof-mark more obvious.

Added proof it was a cow came in the form of its droppings. Fargo examined them and saw that the animal was being fed dry grain regularly, a luxury denied the cow's wilder cousins.

The ruts left by the wheels were a story in themselves. Their depth showed how overburdened the wagon was. Many settlers made the mistake of packing everything they owned, from grandfather clocks to immense stoves, with the result being that their teams had to pull two to three times as much weight as they should. Many animals never made it across the plains; they collapsed and died from sheer exhaustion.

This particular wagon was a large Conestoga, not one of the lighter prairie schooners so popular with settlers bound for a new life in the vast West. Six oxen were toiling under the hot sun to bring it to its destination. Footprints indicated the owner was walking beside the last animal on the left, which was customary.

Frowning, Fargo rose. It bothered him, these people heading into the Badlands. Maybe they were lost. Maybe they had strayed off one of the regular trails and were searching for a town. But if so, why were they traveling south instead of west? Were they on their way to Texas? It was the only explanation he could think of, yet they were going about it all wrong. No one ever took the Badlands route.

Debating what to do, Fargo forked leather. The Conestoga had gone by no more than an hour ago. He could easily catch up and warn them what they were in for, then be on his way. Clucking to the

Ovaro, he started to do just that, then stopped again at the sight of a new set of tracks.

Fargo's first thought was that an Indian was shadowing the greenhorns, but the prints had been made by shod hooofs. It was a white man, on horseback, pacing the wagon. Kneeing his stallion forward, Fargo saw where the horseman had ridden in close to the man guiding the oxen, perhaps to confer, then gone back to his original position ten yards out.

To keep watch for hostiles, Fargo guessed. As seasoned travelers would do. Whoever they were, they apparently knew what they were doing. They must have a reason for venturing into the Badlands. He saw no reason to go on.

Lifting the reins, Fargo was about to resume his interrupted journey when a garish splash of bright color caught his eye. He moved closer, bending low over the pinto's side with his arm extended so he could snag an object partially hidden in the high grass.

It was a doll. A child's plaything, with floppy red curls and a cute painted face and a dress made of gingham. Tiny little cotton shoes had been added. There was even a yellow bow in the hair, a nice touch that hinted at the love the doll's maker bore the doll's owner.

There Fargo sat, a tall muscular man, as rugged as the harsh land around him, bronzed by the sun to where he could pass for a Sioux warrior were it not for his beard, holding the dainty doll in his calloused hand. Pushing his hat brim back, he pondered. His gaze drifted to the southwest, in the general direction of Arizona, his destination. Then it swiveled to the south.

"Damn."

The Ovaro pricked its ears and twisted its neck to regard him closely. It could read his intentions almost as well as Fargo read sign. Small wonder, given how long they had been together. Fargo's wanderlust had taken them from the mighty Mississippi to the broad Pacific, from the baked deserts of Mexico to the frigid woodlands of Canada. He'd sooner part with an arm or leg than his dependable mount.

A light flick of the reins was all it took to send the pinto trotting after the Conestoga. Shifting, Fargo placed the doll in his saddlebags. The presence of a child changed everything. He had to let the party know the dangers they were letting themselves in for. Whether they heeded the warning was up to them. At least he could ride on afterward with a clear conscience.

No one had any business taking a little girl into the Badlands. If thirst didn't get them, hostiles might. Roving bands of Comanches, Kiowa, and Cheyenne passed through the region often, either hunting buffalo or on raids. Then there were the whites who haunted the desolate wilds, badmen every bit as vicious as the land itself, men on the dodge, cutthroats who would as soon dry-gulch unwary innocents as look at them.

Fargo held to a brisk pace until the grassy flatland blended into a series of low gypsum hills that marked the unofficial boundary of the Badlands. The wagon had wound in among them, but Fargo rode to the top of the highest to scout the countryside. Ahead lay blistered terrain that looked as if it had been hacked at by a giant with a gigantic hoe. Not so much as an insect stirred. No birds sang. No deer or antelope or buffalo were to be seen. The land appeared as dead as a corpse.

It didn't help any that the day was unbearably hot. By Fargo's reckoning, the temperature had to be in the upper nineties. The scorched air was as lifeless as everything else. His skin prickled as he descended to the wagon ruts and paralleled them deeper into the muggy heart of the godforsaken emptiness.

Shrub trees and scrub brush were the exception rather than the rule. Occasional tracts of dying grass offered feeble grazing. There wasn't any sign of water but Fargo wasn't worried. He was adept at finding it where most men couldn't. Yet another of the many skills that had earned him the nickname Trailsman.

Suddenly, Fargo stiffened. Wispy tendrils rose from a small valley beyond the hills. It was unlikely the pilgrims had made camp so early, so the smoke must have a more sinister source. Comanches weren't above burning the wagon and all its contents—after disposing of the occupants, of course.

Yanking his Henry from the saddle scabbard, Fargo brought the stallion to a gallop. He worked the trigger guard to lever a round into the chamber. Hugging the base of the last hill, he slowed as the valley unfolded before him. A string of cotton-woods and oaks pinpointed the location of a stream halfway across.

The smoke rose from among the trees. To reach the spot unseen, Fargo veered to the left and circled around. It delayed him but it couldn't be helped. To blunder headlong into a Comanche war party would be asking for an early grave.

Once among the cottonwoods Fargo drew rein to listen. Instead of the yips of warriors or the screams of victims, he heard faint womanish mirth.

Not taking anything for granted, Fargo advanced until movement near the stream let him know he was close enough to be seen. Sliding down, he looped the reins around a trunk. As silent as a stalking cat, he glided along until he saw a small fire. The wagon was parked in shade, the oxen and the cow grazing. A burly man in homespun clothes was inspecting the harness. Near the fire knelt a woman in a plain dress and bonnet, who was consoling a girl of about seven or eight years old.

They were perfectly fine. Fargo lowered the Henry, feeling slightly sheepish. All the effort he had gone to on their behalf, and they behaved as if they were on a Sunday jaunt back in the States.

At the rear of the wagon another figure material-ized, a lithe shape that swung to the ground in the billowy flare of a burgundy dress and a dazzling swirl of golden tresses. A woman of nineteen or twenty, a beauty who would turn the head of any man, held aloft a bundle and called out, "I found it, Ma."

"Fetch it here, Mary Beth," the woman at the fire responded. "Your sister needs something to cheer her up."

Mary Beth obeyed, a lively spring to her step, an alluring sway to her hips. High cheekbones, rosy lips, and a teardrop chin added to her loveliness. "Here you go, Claire Marie," she said to the little girl. "This will take your mind off Sally May."

Fargo idly wondered why they were so fond of saying the first and middle names. The oldest daughter handed the bundle to the mother, who promptly unwrapped a woolen swath and held out the object she uncovered.

"Remember this one, Claire Marie? You called her Patricia Jane. She was the first you ever owned."

It was another doll, smaller than the one Fargo found, with stringy brown hair that crowned a pair of button eyes and a cross-stitched mouth. A tattered dress testified to the heavy use the doll had seen.

Clair sniffled and shook her head. "I don't want this old one, Ma! I want Sally May! She's special."

The mother sadly rested a hand on her youngest daughter's shoulder. "I'm sorry, child, but we can't go back to look for it. There's no telling where you lost it."

"You have only yourself to blame," threw in Mary Beth. "Ma told you time and time again not to sit at the very back of the wagon, that you might fall out or drop something. But you wouldn't listen."

"Now, now, Mary Beth," the mother said. "You'll only make your sister feel worse."

The girl already did. Tears welled up as Claire declared, "You're mean, Mary! I didn't drop her! I think I lost her when we hit that big bump!"

Fargo could end the child's suffering. Cradling the Henry, he approached their camp. Typical of greenhorns, no one spotted him until he was almost on top of them. Then the oldest daughter, Mary Beth, looked up and gasped in alarm. Their mother leaped up, snatching the smaller girl to her bosom. All three gasped in dismay, as if he were a Kiowa painted for war.

"Who the devil are you, mister?" Mary Beth recovered her wits first.

"A friend," Fargo said.

Anxiety etched the mother's features. Tilting her head, she shouted, "Edward! Edward! There's a stranger here!"

The man pivoted. He had a square jaw, bushy brows, and hands the size of hams. Hurrying over, he mustered a wary smile, the smile of a man who had been caught with his guard down and was hoping his negligence wouldn't cost his loved ones their lives. "Howdy, friend," he said earnestly, thrusting out one of those oversized hands. "Edward Webber, at your service. This is my family."

Fargo shook, gave his name, and further put them at ease by saying, "I came across your trail a while back and was worried you might run into trouble."

"Aren't you from Paradise?" Edward asked.

"Where?"

"The town we're headed to," the settler said, then introduced the others.

The wife's name was Esther. She set Claire down once she was assured Fargo posed no threat, and said, "Would you care for some coffee? I was just about to put some on, and we'd be delighted to have you join us. Your company is most welcome. Other than Mr. Vetch, we haven't seen a living soul in weeks."

"Count yourself lucky," Fargo mentioned. "This is Indian country. If you're on your way to Texas, you're well west of where you should be."

Edward Webber shook his head. "Paradise isn't in Texas."

There was that name again. In all Fargo's wide-flung travels, he's never heard of it. But then, new settlements were springing up all the time. "Where is it? Eastern Arizona?"

"No, no," Edward said, chuckling. "It's not more than a two-day ride from here."

"Paradise is in the *Badlands*?" Fargo couldn't keep the shock from his voice. As near as he knew, the wastelands were as empty of habitation as they were of everything else. Surely he'd have heard if a town had been started up. It would be the talk of every saloon from Denver to Santa Fe.

Edward's bushy brows knit. "What are the Badlands?"

To say Fargo was flabbergasted would not do his astonishment justice. He was well aware that far too many settlers were woefully ignorant of life in the West, but this beat all. Most never bothered to learn about the wildlife or Indians or anything else of importance. They just loaded up their belongings and traipsed off to the Promised Land with complete confidence Providence would spare them from harm.

Here was a sterling example. A man who had brought his family into one of the worst regions in the whole country, and he *didn't even know where he was*. Some people, Fargo mused, were dumber than the beasts of burden they relied on to get them where they were going. "The name speaks for itself." Fargo gestured. "And you're in them."

The eldest daughter, Mary Beth, had been listening attentively while studying Fargo on the sly. He'd noticed her admiring the width of his shoulders, and he inwardly grinned when she let her eyes linger lower down. "If that's true," she broke in, "how come Mr. Vetch never mentioned it?"

"Who is this Vetch character?" Fargo inquired.

"Cyrus Vetch," Edward Webber elaborated. "He came along when we needed him most. Our wagon had lost a wheel and I couldn't get the spare on by myself. If not for him, we'd still be stranded in the middle of the Kansas prairie."

"He's from Paradise," Mary Beth said. "The owner of the general store there. He was one of the first to stake a claim, and he's helped to make the town a thriving success.

"In the *Badlands*?" Fargo repeated. Maybe he was unwilling to believe it, he reflected, because it confirmed what he had long feared. That one day settlers would swarm over the West like a plague of locusts, overrunning it with homesteads and towns and cities until there wasn't a square foot of wilderness left. All the wild beasts and the Indians and open spaces would be gone, and with them the way of life that Fargo loved.

Here was evidence it might really happen. If settlers could put down roots in the Badlands, they could put down roots *anywhere*. No place was safe, not the highest peak or the remotest valley. It was the beginning of the end.

Mary Beth chuckled, a silken, throaty bubbling, like rapids over rocks, full of vitality and sensual charm. "You're a strange one, Mr. Fargo. I should think you would be glad for us. Now we don't need to go all the way to Oregon."

"That's right," her father said. "We can take our pick of prime land. Within a year I'll be plowing my own fields, storing grain in my own barn." Edward rubbed his hands in eager anticipation. "Cyrus tells us that he knows of a valley where the grass is green all year. It has a fine spring and plenty of game."

Fargo couldn't help himself from being skeptical, and gazed around the clearing. "Where is this Mr. Vetch? I'd like to meet him."

"Oh, he went off to hunt," Edward said. "We stopped a bit earlier than usual because my wife is feeling poorly. Some venison and a good night's sleep should have her fit as a fiddle by morning."

"Is she sick?" Fargo asked. Certain roots and plants were quite effective in curing aches and ills, and he was versed in their use.

"Not in the way you mean," Edward said, glancing at his wife, who was rummaging in the back of the wagon. He nodded at his oldest daughter, who had been gawking at Fargo the whole time, as if there were more he wanted to say but couldn't with her present. Fargo's confusion must have shown because Edward added, "Once a month or so we have the same problem."

Mary Beth blushed. "Pa!"

Now it was Fargo's turn to chuckle. "That's all right. I'm a grown man. You're a grown woman. What's the harm?"

Her blush deepened. Scooping up her younger sister, Mary Beth flounced toward the wagon, sniping over a shoulder, "There are some subjects that should never be talked about in front of a lady. If Ma found out, she'd blister your ears, Pa."

Edward Webber sighed. "Women. We can't live without them, and we can't live with them. What's a fellow to do?"

Fargo's chuckle became a belly laugh. He bent forward, holding his side, and in doing so he inadvertently saved his life. For as he did, a rifle cracked and a slug buzzed so close about his head that it nudged his hat. Instantly, Fargo flung himself flat, then rolled, bringing the Henry up and around with the stock pressed to his shoulder. Edward was imitating a stupefied ox. The women had frozen in amazement.

"Get down!" Fargo hollered.

The rifleman in the trees fired again. Gunsmoke puffed skyward as the bullet thudded in the earth at Fargo's elbow. He banged off two swift shots in reply, aiming at the smoke, and he must have come close because a vague shape retreated into the brush. In a twinkling, Fargo heaved upright and gave chase, bellowing at the pilgrims, "Take cover under the wagon!"

The bushwhacker was in full flight.

Fargo weaved among the cottonwoods, eager for a clear shot. He caught a glimpse of a man in buckskins. Without warning, the bushwhacker whirled and snapped off another shot, forcing Fargo to dive behind a tree. It bought the would-be killer a few precious seconds.

Swearing, Fargo pushed to his feet and resumed his pursuit. They were bearing due east, along the north bank of the stream, where cover was heaviest. Twice he almost fired, but in each instance he didn't have a clear enough shot.

Who could it be? Fargo wondered. A lone warrior out to slay a white for the sheer hell of it? Possibly, but Fargo was doubtful. Warriors generally roved in war parties, not singly. Was it a white man—a badman—then? Maybe. But, like warriors, they tended to travel in groups.

The only other prospect Fargo could think of was the mystery man, Cyrus Vetch. So far as Fargo knew, Vetch was the only other person within fifty miles. But why would Vetch try to put a window in his skull? What did the man hope to gain?

Another slug, shattering a low limb close to Fargo's right ear, put an end to his speculation. He had let his mind stray at the worst possible moment. Angry at himself, he answered in kind, not once but twice, a waste of lead since he couldn't see his target.

Feet drummed dully. Fargo closed on the sound, narrowing the gap. He was no more than forty or fifty feet from his quarry when a horse nickered. Pumping his legs faster, he spied its silhouette outlined against the background of green growth. He also saw the bushwhacker clambering onto the saddle. Again Fargo brought up the Henry, but as he fixed a hasty bead the man slapped his legs and the horse bolted around a wide oak. Thwarted, Fargo listened to the cracking and crashing fade in the distance, then he jerked his rifle down and turned on a boot heel.

The bastard had gotten clean away! Fargo was tempted to go after him, to track the man down no matter how long it took. But that would mean leaving the Webber family on their own, and he was reluctant to part company until he had learned more about Paradise—and Cyrus Vetch.

Hiking to the Ovaro, Fargo stepped into the stirrups and rode to their camp. They had done as he instructed and were huddled under the Conestoga, Edward and Esther armed with rifles, Mary Beth with the Walker Colt. Their relief at seeing him alive was genuine. They bustled out as he slid down.

Much to Fargo's surprise, Mary Beth put a warm hand on his arm and gave a soft squeeze. "Thank God you weren't hurt! All that shooting! We feared the worst."

"Did you see who it was?" Esther wanted to know.

"A skulking savage, I'll wager," Edward declared.

"Vetch warned us there are a few in this neck of the woods."

Fargo was making it a habit to repeat half of what the farmer said. "Just a few?" Tying the pinto to the wagon bed, he shoved the Henry into the scabbard. "Half the warriors in the Comanche nation pass through this area two or three times a year." He turned to his saddlebags.

Edward snorted. "Surely you exaggerate, friend. Cyrus guaranteed me the countryside around Paradise is as safe as Illinois. He told us the last Indian attacks took place over a decade ago."

Fargo wanted to say that Vetch was an idiot but he refrained. As a general rule he never insulted someone unless he could do so to his face. "I almost forgot," he said, undoing the straps. "I have something that belongs to one of you."

Claire let out with a delighted squeal when Fargo showed her the doll. She beamed and hugged it close, then startled Fargo by clasping his legs and giving him the same affectionate treatment.

"Thank you, Mr. Fargo! Thank you, thank you, thank you! Sally May is my best friend in all the world!"

Mary Beth snickered. "It's just a silly doll. But the way you carry on, a body would think it was flesh and blood."

Esther Webber pointed at her oldest. "You have no room to talk, missy. As I recall, there was a doll you were fond of when you were Claire Marie's age. Gladys, you called her, and you wouldn't go to bed at night unless she was tucked at your side."

Mary blushed again. "I didn't know any better back then. I was only a kid."

"And what do you think your sister is?" Esther countered.

Edward motioned at the fire. "How about that coffee we promised you, Mr. Fargo? We'd be honored if you'd stick around. Maybe stay the night if you're so inclined." He paused. "Besides, Mr. Vetch is bound to return before too long and you can lean all about Paradise firsthand."

Fargo's gaze drifted across the clearing, then from the father to the mother to the oldest daughter. As a Texan might say, she was as fine a filly as he had ever set eyes on, her full breasts seeming to strain against her dress like ripe fruit fit to burst. The enticing swell of her thighs was added incentive. "I'll take you up on your offer, Ed."

The family was in fine spirits. They chattered like chipmunks, grateful that Fargo had saved them. They thought all was well, but Fargo knew better. The killer who had opened fire on them might come back—with friends.

Acting relaxed but always alert, Fargo sipped the delicious coffee Mrs. Webber made and answered a hundred and one questions about everything from the change of seasons to the migration of buffalo.

Edward, in particular, was interested in anything that had a bearing on farming. Blazing bands of red, orange, and vivid yellow painted the western sky when he stretched and commented, "The sun will be going down in half an hour. I can't imagine where Mr. Vetch has gotten to."

"What does he look like?" Fargo asked, expecting Ed to say that Vetch wore buckskins, too.

"Oh, he's a roly-poly gent with a smile that would melt butter. About the friendliest human being I've ever met. He wears store-boughten clothes, a gray jacket and pants and a white shirt. And a fancy gray bowler."

Esther tittered. "Please don't tell him I said this, but Cyrus is quite comical. He makes me think of the circus clown we saw over at Hartford that time we visited my sister."

"We're from Illinois," Ed remarked.

Fargo had already deduced as much. He was more interested in the description of their kindly benefactor. Based on their description, it couldn't possibly have been Vetch who tried to make wolf meat of him. "I'm looking forward to meeting your friend," he said, reaching for the coffeepot.

Just then, to the west, a wavering shriek fluttered on the wind, the horrified wail of someone suffering anguish beyond measure.